Gianfranco Calligarich
LAST SUMMER IN THE CITY
Translated by Howard Curtis

Gianfranco Calligarich was born in Asmara, Eritrea, and grew up in Milan, then moved to Rome, where he worked as a journalist and screenwriter. He wrote many successful TV shows for Rai, the national public broadcasting company of Italy, and founded the Teatro XX Secolo in 1994. He is the author of many novels, including *La malinconia dei Crusich*, which won the Viareggio-Rèpaci Prize. *Last Summer in the City* is the first of his novels to be translated into English.

Howard Curtis lives in Norwich, England, and has translated more than a hundred books from the French, Italian, and Spanish.

LAST SUMMER
IN THE CITY

LAST SUMMER IN THE CITY

GIANFRANCO CALLIGARICH

Translated from the Italian by Howard Curtis

Foreword by André Aciman

PICADOR   FARRAR, STRAUS AND GIROUX   NEW YORK

Picador

120 Broadway, New York 10271

Copyright © 2016 by Bompiani / Rizzoli Libri S.p.A., Milano

Translation copyright © 2021 by Howard Curtis

Foreword copyright © 2021 by André Aciman

All rights reserved

Printed in the United States of America

Originally published in Italian in 2016 by Bompiani / Rizzoli Libri S.p.A.,
Italy, as *L'ultima Estate in Città*

English translation published in the United States in 2021 by Farrar, Straus
and Giroux

First paperback edition, 2022

Frontispiece photograph by Catarina Belova / Shutterstock.com.

The Library of Congress has cataloged the Farrar, Straus and Giroux hardcover
edition as follows:

Names: Calligarich, Gianfranco, author. | Curtis, Howard, 1949– translator.

Title: Last summer in the city / Gianfranco Calligarich ; translated from the
Italian by Howard Curtis.

Other titles: Ultima estate in città. English

Description: First American edition. | New York : Farrar, Straus and Giroux,
2021. | Originally published in Italian in 2016 Bompiani / Rizzoli Libri S.p.A.,
Italy, as L'ultima Estate in Città.

Identifiers: LCCN 2021010522 | ISBN 9780374600150 (hardcover)

Classification: LCC PQ4863.A3837 U513 2021 | DDC 853/.914—dc23

LC record available at https://lccn.loc.gov/2021010522

Paperback ISBN: 978-1-250-84925-0

Designed by Janet Evans-Scanlon

Our books may be purchased in bulk for promotional, educational, or
business use. Please contact your local bookseller or the Macmillan Corporate
and Premium Sales Department at 1-800-221-7945, extension 5442, or by email
at MacmillanSpecialMarkets@macmillan.com.

Picador® is a U.S. registered trademark and is used by Macmillan Publishing
Group, LLC, under license from Pan Books Limited.

For book club information, please visit facebook.com/picadorbookclub or
email marketing@picadorusa.com.

picadorusa.com • instagram.com/picador
twitter.com/picadorusa • facebook.com/picadorusa

10   9   8   7   6

To Sara Calligarich

The first great disaster to befall mankind
was not the flood but the drying out.

—SÁNDOR FERENCZI

                              As he rose and fell
He passed the stages of his age and youth
Entering the whirlpool.

—T. S. ELIOT

FOREWORD

By André Aciman

Last Summer in the City, by the Italian novelist, playwright, and screenwriter Gianfranco Calligarich, was first published in 1973. He had arrived in Rome in his early twenties as a correspondent for a small newspaper based in Milan, and not much later, when recalled to Milan by the paper, decided instead to stay in Rome to devote himself to a novel, probably his plan all along. When finished, however, the book was turned down by every Italian publisher until dropping into the hands of one of Italy's most renowned writers and essayists, Natalia Ginzburg. She read it overnight, and her response was so enthusiastic that she got the publishing house Garzanti, which was initially underwhelmed by the novel, to publish it. Seventeen thousand copies were sold that summer, earning the young author a *succès d'estime* as well as a book prize. But not much later, the novel disappeared from the shelves and could be found only in scattered bookstalls and secondhand bookstores around Italy. Copies, however, were vigorously coveted by booklovers and reading groups, including some doctoral students, and the novel became the object of a cult among the literary cognoscenti. Then, nearly four decades later, in 2010, the prestigious small publishing house Nino Aragno Editore decided to reissue *Last Summer*. Deemed once again a highly crafted and serious novel, it was reviewed to great acclaim, with many critics openly kicking themselves for neglecting Calligarich's work when it was first published. But once again, and despite being reviewed by almost all of Italy's main dailies, the novel dropped from sight, only to be finally rereleased in 2016 by Bompiani as well as by a number of international publishing houses.

Calligarich is not a familiar Italian surname. It has Slovenian and Serbo-Croatian roots, and, like many surnames ending in *ich*, is frequently claimed by Italo-Slovenians whose lineage most likely goes back to the port city of Trieste. Many Italians continue to keep the Slavic surnames without necessarily feeling any connection to a Slavic ancestry.

But Gianfranco Calligarich's origins are more complex. He was born in Asmara, Eritrea, once a thriving Italian colony. His father, who was born in Corfu to a Greek mother and a Triestine father, was Jewish, while his wife was Piedmontese. Gianfranco himself grew up in Milan, then moved to Rome, and yet, as he claimed in an interview, his roots are planted in Trieste, where he would most likely want to be buried. His extended family feels drawn to Trieste, dreams Trieste, feels Trieste, and ultimately claims to belong to no place but Trieste, even if many of its members may never have set foot there and wouldn't begin to understand the Italian spoken by native Triestini. His grandfather's life is worthy of a tiny epic, since the man, born with Slavic roots, moved from Trieste to Corfu, married a Greek woman, and later, on being branded a deserter by the Austro-Hungarian Army during World War I, fled on the first ship he found, landed in Italy, and settled in Milan. On his deathbed—or so the story goes in *Last Summer in the City*—Calligarich's grandfather, who had traveled the seas in his younger days and whose mind was already drifting to a seagirt Trieste of memory, asks his son to let him taste some seawater. Though the request may seem strange, coming as it did in landlocked Milan, his son, in Calligarich's novel, has no choice but to get in his car and drive all the way to Genoa with his fourteen-year-old son, whose brooding silence seems to have become the norm. The boy's father finally reaches the sea, fills up a bottle with water, and drives all the way back to Milan only to find his dying father already unconscious. Still, the dutiful son, who could very well be Gianfranco's father, daubs his father's face with the salty water even if the dying man is past caring or being grateful for the gesture.

Seawater is not in the slightest insignificant, since Leo Gazzara, the narrator of the novel, who at times could probably be a stand-in for the author himself, will choose to leave Milan and move to Rome, in good part because of its proximity to the beach. There are, in the novel, numberless times when, on a lark, the narrator will hop in his car and drive for a good half hour to the sea. Trieste, after all, faces the sea, and finding the sea anywhere on the planet remains, in more ways than one, a form of homecoming for the narrator. His Triestine grandfather found closure by asking for seawater, and, fifteen years later, at the age of thirty, Leo will too.

Diving into the sea or just walking along the shoreline remains a source of undiminished bliss and purifying solace for Leo, a moment when his persistent penury, failures, defeats, and the unyielding solitude that he struggles to flee as obstinately as he keeps seeking it out all are summarily wiped off by a sudden plunge underwater, an instance of physical and spiritual redemption that this young man is unable to find elsewhere. "I dived in and swam until I was out of breath. Then I turned and played dead, listening to the swish of the water around my ears. I felt good, I couldn't remember ever feeling that good."

This, in many ways, could be the very best that life has to offer Leo Gazzara. He fritters away his days and nights in Rome, on sleepless hours with Arianna or in tumultuous all-night benders with his pal Graziano, while all he's desperately trying to do is reshuffle the worthless cards that life has dealt him. In this, as so many critics were all too quick to point out, he is the incarnation of Marcello Rubini of *La Dolce Vita* (1960) and now, with the wisdom of hindsight, of Jep Gambardella of *La Grande Bellezza* (2013). Both films are about the aimless lives of well-heeled journalists whose careers were taken over by worldly ambitions when in truth their deeper vocation was literature, a dream destined to be perpetually postponed if not altogether shelved. As colorful as Marcello's life may seem, the shallow itinerary of his day-to-day is a perpetual skidding from one woman to another, one nightclub after another, one gathering, one soirée, one person, to the next. Gambardella's itinerary is hardly different. Clearly inspired by Fellini's classic from fifty-plus years earlier, Sorrentino's *The Great Beauty* is a far less somber portrait of the decadent lifestyle of the privileged few and reflects an Italy that moved on following its startling postwar boom of the early sixties, then survived the *Anni di piombo* of the seventies and eighties—the "Years of Lead," when Italy faced an endless assault of political carnage that eventually claimed the life of Prime Minister Aldo Moro in 1978—only to come out as elegantly disenchanted and unflappably put-together, but no less feckless and disaffected, than the sixties Rome of Fellini's speckling Via Veneto. As Jep chastises Stefania in the famous balcony scene, "We're all on the brink of despair." This never changes. It sits on every page of Calligarich's novel. His characters, unless gainfully employed or blinkered by upward mobility, sit on the brink of despair, condemned, as each is, to a staring contest with the abyss, sensing all along that the abyss is winning. What holds them together, what feeds and enables their internal atrophy, is Rome itself.

The Rome of the early seventies is not just a city with famous sites and monuments, most of which are to this very day still begrimed by age and neglect. Rome is where almost everyone in *Last Summer* charts his or her circuitous transit through a city that, despite claiming a historic center, has no center and lets everyone feel squandered and scattered about. All Leo does is drift—as Arianna, his love interest, drifts; as Graziano, his drunken friend, drifts; as Fellini's Marcello drifts. People don't amble or stroll in Rome, they meander, and stray from the Spanish Steps to Piazza Navona, to Campo de' Fiori, over and across Ponte Sisto to Trastevere, then back across the river to Piazza del Popolo, Via Frattina, and finally once again to Piazza di Spagna and Trinità dei Monti. Places spill into one another, by turns splendid and beautiful, then ordinary and drab, mirroring Calligarich's masterful prose style, which frequently jolts the highly elegiac with the brutally colloquial.

Calligarich's Rome is lived and loved in all seasons, at all hours of the day and night, dawn especially. Not a city easy to peel off or to abandon and forget. And to bring the point home, Calligarich quotes Cavafy's unforgettable poem:

> *There is no ship for you, there is no road*
> *As you have destroyed your life here*
> *in this little corner, you have ruined it in the entire world.*
>
> (TRANSLATION BY RAE DALVEN)

And yet, as Calligarich has Arianna say, no one is from Rome. Everyone comes from elsewhere. Rome is home to the transient, to those who don't belong anywhere, who are unfinished, who have a self but want another and can't, for the life of them, disown the one they've got. They drift and they ramble. One way or another, they will ultimately *alzare le vele*—to use a common phrase in the novel—hoist their sails, or, as more accurately rendered here, get the hell out.

One learns to hate Rome so as to stop loving it.

Or it's the other way around: one loves it because one could easily hate it.

Rome is the lingering, glamorous patina that blinds the characters of *Last Summer in the City* to the very real fact that they are seriously damaged and marooned. Despite their few moments of mirth and pleasure, each is an emotional cripple. What afflicts them all, if observed from a purely literary perspective, is a classic case of existential anomie. Whether they are rich or poor, settled or not, with or without someone who means anything to them, all seem to spin their wheels. There is no one to blame, everyone to scorn, and only one person to love—if you could even call it love, because the feeling bristles with so many barbs that one should know enough to leave it alone. Better to flee and leave everything behind.

Booze is an option, and Leo is prey to alcohol and will stop drinking only after being stricken with the DTs. Friendship is another option, as are women; then there are books, the sea, and finally, of course, as ever again, beloved Rome, home to the abyss. Rome cradles all forms of dejection, nourishes them, and then, when you least suspect it, turns out to have been starving you all along. Calligarich's characters, and Leo in particular, are unwilling or unable to connect with others, to consummate whatever life tosses their way. While they may be dissolute, ultimately they are numb to experience itself. This is neo-Sartre and post-Camus. As his friend Graziano will tell Leo, "You can't just go on like this."

But, yes, he can. And his curse is that he knows he can.

What gives him the greatest pleasure is not so much sleeping with a woman but waking up in her bed after she has gone to work and smelling the coffee, ready to be reheated, or, better yet, getting up, roaming around the empty apartment, switching on music, reheating the coffee, then finally lounging in a bathtub filled with hot water. After which he'll dry himself with clean towels, dress, and shut the door behind him, never to return. Women, as he himself says, come easily to him.

Then one evening Leo meets the beautiful Arianna. They're at a stylish cocktail party in a large apartment owned by a friend who is a successful television producer who will eventually offer Leo a job, though within a few hours of being hired Leo will walk out. With hardly a penny to his name, and soaked from a rainstorm, Leo arrives at the party, where people are very consciously bedecked in fashionable rainy-day clothes. A rolling cart containing various alcoholic beverages makes the rounds. And a bowl full of peanuts materializes. Totally famished, Leo tackles the peanuts. When the hostess, his friend, asks him to fetch some ice from the kitchen—it's their butler's evening off— Leo opens the refrigerator and gorges himself on all manner of cheeses. On his way to and from the kitchen he runs into Arianna, who is curled up on the floor, on the phone. They talk for a moment, then reconnect later, and eventually, by three in the morning, leave together. They casually talk books; she loves Proust. She asks him when he would have liked to be born. His answer: "In Vienna before the end of the empire." Perhaps his is an unconscious wish to walk back his family tree to a time preceding his grandfather's flight from the Austro-Hungarian Empire, when everything was as it should be, or so it seems in retrospect. As for Arianna, her answer to the same question couldn't be simpler: "Combray," she says.

Then she asks him to drive her to the Capitol. "'I'd like to see the city from the terraces of the Capitoline Hill.' We got there in five minutes and went and leaned on the parapet just above the Forum. Beneath us, the squares were deserted, and the basilicas, frozen in marble, were dreaming of the day they would thaw." At which point she utters something that underwrites the source of Leo's—and one is tempted to assume Calligarich's own—malaise. "'Feeling nostalgic for something we never had.'"

Leo and Arianna feel like throwbacks from an almost remembered era that may never have been but that beckons to a better life that is indeed their rightful life, not the one they're given in this makeshift town called Rome. His reply to her sudden exclamation will come a few pages later when they end up having brioches at dawn, and he remembers it's his birthday. He is thirty years old, and, raising his boiling cup of *caffellatte* as though it were a champagne glass, he toasts, "'To all the things we haven't done, the things we should have done, and the things we won't do.'"

Neither belongs either here or elsewhere, either in this calendar year or any other year.

No two stranded souls could have been better paired—which is why they are terminally destructive.

We may, barring another name for it, call this love.

It springs on them at the bus station, among the rising "good smell of coffee, that good smell cafés have early in the morning."

But they won't speak a word of love. Instead, she asks him to drive her to the sea. They'll walk on the shore, close to the waves, feel the weather turn chilly, he'll hold her, she'll hold him, and Arianna will keep testing him throughout the night. But no sex, she warns. She will eventually fall in love with him, but in the past tense, "'God, how I loved you . . . How I loved you,'" she'll confide one day, and he too will say much the same, "'I think I'm in love with you,'" to which she will snap back, "'Never say that again.'"

Then they start kissing, and when he asks her to come home with him she says, "*Are you crazy? . . .* I don't feel like making love, haven't you got that yet?" and he narrates, "She gave me a last, light kiss on the lips."

Leo will struggle not to speak his love, and almost drives himself into believing he feels no love for her, while she has been running hot and cold with him, until, maybe all too suddenly, in bed together, he realizes he is unable to feel aroused and longs for the warmth that would have stirred him: "I was frozen and unhappy and there was nothing in me, not even a little of that warmth I would have liked more than anything else in my life, that all-consuming warmth that would have spread from my belly through my body so that in the end I'd be able to reach her." Much later in the novel, when she is emotionally available to him, he longs not for that *tepore* (warmth) in his belly but for exactly the opposite, *torpore* (numbness): ". . . the languor I had so long looked for with her." The paradox couldn't be crueler. And yet, as unsettling as this paradox can be, it is compounded by another paradox far more bitter and harder to swallow when Leo realizes that Arianna is now living with another man: "I felt she was mine," Leo thinks, four pages before the end of the novel. "I had never before felt that so much as I did now, when she was someone else's. What lousy luck. I knew what it meant, that she could only belong to me when she was someone else's."

Avanzo *in Italian means a leftover, a remnant, the unwanted, dis-*carded remains of someone else's life or property. In many ways, that one word also sums up the essence of Leo's life. From a cheap hotel near Campo de' Fiori, he moves into his married friends' apartment when they invite him to house-sit during their two-year absence in Mexico. Their marriage is on the rocks, and they welcome the change of scenery; Leo makes a pass at the wife, when the husband is not in the room, but things don't go any further. Since the couple can't take their old Alfa Romeo abroad with them, they sell it to him for a pittance. The car, the apartment on Monte Mario, down to the bowl of peanuts at the party, even the attempted pass at the wife—all these details, as Leo will grow increasingly aware, are leftovers from other people's lives.

Similarly, though married to an American millionairess, the perpetually drunken Graziano Castelvecchio loves to dine on *avanzi* in restaurants. Some restaurants, he claims, have the best *avanzi*.

It is, however, Graziano who dots the *i*'s to what remains a dominant key in Leo's life. He, like Graziano, is a leftover, a survivor of an extinct species. "'Look around you,' he said as we walked down Via del Corso, surrounded by people coming out of office buildings. 'Is there anything you feel part of? No, there isn't. And you know why there isn't? Because we belong to an extinct species. We happen to still be alive, that's all,' he said, stopping to light a cigar. Because, if I didn't know, we were born just when beautiful old Europe was fine-tuning its most lucid, thorough, and definitive suicide attempt."

Yes, there is more than a touch of self-pity and drama in that statement, but it bites through the novel with sharp teeth, because the truth that even the novel doesn't see clearly enough is that all those who work in offices and, as Leo is quick to notice, look sprightly and busy cradling their lit pipes in their hands, even they feel like survivors of a long-extinct species. They may not realize it, and may be hiding it from themselves and from everyone else, which is why the novel speaks to everyone, which is why everyone is ultimately a self-identifying existentialist, even when we feel ridiculous admitting it and can so easily trace our own profile in a novel steeped in malaise and ennui. No one *belongs*, but everyone is persuaded that everyone else *belongs*. The truth is, we are, each of us, perpetually alone. It is difficult to determine whether what devastates us more is knowing that we are condemned to perpetual solitude or thinking we have been singled out to confront and then deplore our solitude. Leo and Graziano are like two soon-to-be fossils roaming the surface of planet Earth. "If I were a fag, I'd fall in love with you. Wouldn't we make a lovely couple?" Graziano says. But here is the ultimate bummer: "We'll turn gay and then at least we'll be something. This way, what are we now? We're nothing, not even fags."

There was a moment when Leo was persuaded that except for Arianna, everything else he touched was destined to be an *avanzo*. But then, just when he believed she was in his life, he discovers that she too, like everything else in his life, is an *avanzo*—in this case, an *avanzo* from another man's bed.

"*Che sfiga*," he thinks when he finally realizes that the woman he loves is now headed to that other man.

Sfiga means bad luck, the way *sfigato* means inept, unlucky, loser, downright pitiful, a word that coincides with another word that pullulates in the novel as well, *sfinocchiato*, meaning dejected, exhausted, fucked-up. These are signature words in this novel, and there is no doubt that Leo is pursued by bad luck and a paralyzing sense of inadequacy. There is no escape. Something grabs ahold of him and won't let go until it chokes him, because, to paraphrase Cavafy, having ruined his life in this little corner, he has destroyed it in the whole world.

On Christmas Day, feeling completely disconnected and stranded in Rome, Leo Gazzara boards a train headed for Milan. Like Ulysses, who finally wakes up in Ithaca but fails to recognize his homeland now that two decades have elapsed, Leo has some difficulty identifying the street where he grew up. So much had changed during his short absence. But then having found his bearings, he spots his father leaving their building and getting into his car. Upstairs, from a window, his mother is watching her husband, while he gestures for her to get back inside and shut it, for fear of catching a cold. Leo has half a mind to put his arm under his father's and surprise him, but then he hesitates and decides against it. He had planned to spend Christmas with them, but now he realizes that his sisters and their husbands and children, along with his parents, lead lives where someone like him has no place. Why bother them? He buys a sandwich and gets on a train headed back to Rome. But, then, Rome is not home, and neither is Milan, nor, for that matter, is Trieste. They are all mirages, leftovers from the ledger of time and space.

When he returns, he'll eventually hear that the friends who had lent him their apartment are returning from Mexico, and thus, one by one, the cards dealt him are being reshuffled, the good with the bad. He is alone. He moves back to the hotel where he'd been living before his friends' hiatus abroad.

There is only Arianna left, probably the love of his life. And she loves him too. But she lives with someone else now. Then he tells her that Graziano has died. And for the first time since he's known her, she is totally hysterical. She was already weeping because she feared they couldn't have a life together. Now she is inconsolable because death has brutally barged into their lives.

There is nowhere to turn, no one to talk to, nothing to do. He packs up one suitcase with his books, another with his clothes, says good-bye to the porter at his hotel, jumps in his old Alfa Romeo, and knows what he must do. First, he'll have a swim. And maybe at this point he'll remember the words from *The Last of the Mohicans* that he'd read at Graziano's funeral, because they apply to him as well: "My race has gone from the shores of the salt lake and the hills of the Delawares. But who can say that the serpent of his tribe has forgotten his wisdom."

These are the words of Chief Chingachgook, who ends the funeral speech for his son with these three tragic words: "I am alone." Calligarich does not quote "I am alone," but he couldn't be unaware of their dark and brooding presence over his own words. His protagonist too is alone. Indeed, Leo is, has always been, more than just alone.

No language has a word for being more than *just* alone.

LAST SUMMER
IN THE CITY

1

*Anyway, it's always like that. You do your best to keep to your-*self and then one fine day, without knowing how, you find you're caught up in something that sweeps you along with it to the bitter end.

Personally, I would happily have stayed out of the race. I'd known all kinds of people, some who'd reached the finishing post and others who hadn't even gotten off the starting block, and sooner or later they all ended up equally dissatisfied, which is why I'd come to the conclusion that it was better to stay on the sidelines and just observe life. But I hadn't reckoned with being desperately short of money one rainy day at the beginning of spring last year. All the rest followed naturally, as these things do. Let me make it clear from the start that I don't blame anyone, I was dealt my cards and I played them. That's all.

And this bay really is magnificent. It's overlooked by a Saracen fortress on top of a rocky promontory that juts out into the sea for a hundred yards or so. Looking toward the coast, I can see the dazzling spread of beach and the green of the low Mediterranean vegetation. Farther on, a three-lane highway, deserted at this time of year, tunnels into a chain of rocky hills glittering in the sun. The sky is blue, the sea clear.

I couldn't have chosen better, truth be told.

I've always loved the sea. There must have been something in my boyhood tendency to linger on beaches that reflected the impulse that had led my grandfather to spend his youth on Mediterranean merchant ships before landing in Milan, that gloomy city, and cramming an apartment full of children. I knew this grandfather. He was a gray-eyed old Slav who died surrounded by a large number of descendants. The last words he managed to utter were a request for a little seawater, and my father, as the eldest son, left one of my sisters to mind his stamp shop and set off for Genoa in his car. I went with him. I was fourteen, and I remember we didn't say a word for the whole of the ride. My father never talked a lot, and since I was already giving him a few problems with my lack of progress at school, it was in my best interests to keep quiet. It was the shortest of my trips to the sea, just long enough to fill a bottle, but also the most pointless, because by the time we got back Grandpa was almost completely unconscious. My father washed the old man's face with water from the bottle, but Grandpa didn't seem to particularly appreciate it.

A few years later, the fact of the sea being so close was one of the things that drew me to Rome. After my military service, I was faced with the problem of what to do with my life, but the more I looked around, the less I was able to come to a decision. My friends had very clear ideas—graduate, get married, make money—but that was a prospect that repelled me. These were the years when money mattered even more than usual in Milan, the years that saw a kind of nationwide conjuring trick also known as the Economic Boom, and in a way I too benefited from it. It was at this time that a medical-literary magazine for which I occasionally wrote a few well-judged but badly paid articles had the opportunity to open an office in Rome and I was hired as their correspondent.

While my mother used every argument she could to prevent my departure, my father said nothing. He'd silently watched my attempts at social integration, comparing them with the successes of my elder sisters, who at a young age had married white-collar workers, perfectly respectable men, and, as I had done during that trip to get water for my grandfather, I took advantage of his silence to keep quiet myself. He and I never talked. I don't know which of us was to blame—I don't even know if you can talk about blame here—but I always had the feeling that if I'd confronted him directly I would somehow have hurt him. The war had sent him a long way away without sparing him any of its well-known peculiarities. Nobody to whom a thing like that happens can return home exactly as he was before. In spite of his proud silence, it always seemed as if he was trying to make us forget something, perhaps the fact he'd come home a shattered man and had made us watch his big body writhing as the electric shocks shuddered through it. Anyway, that's how he was, and when I was a boy I could never forgive him for his unheroic profession, his love of order, his excessive respect for inanimate things, not understanding what terrible destruction he must have witnessed to then set about repairing an old kitchen chair with infinite patience on the very day he came back from the war. And yet, even now, after almost thirty years, there's still something of the soldier about him, the patience, the tendency to hold his head high, the habit of not asking questions, and even now, if he'd given me nothing else, I'll never forget the fearlessness I felt as a boy walking by his side. Because, even now, the thought of my father's stride is the one thing more than any other that immediately takes me back to my childhood, and even now, even in the green expanse surrounding me, I can return as if by magic to his side, remembering his soft, dusty stride, apparently impervious to fatigue, the stride of those long marches as a soldier, the stride that one way or another he'd somehow managed to bring back home with him.

So I set off for Rome, and everything would have gone perfectly if my father, quite unexpectedly forgoing his own pride, hadn't decided to go with me to the station and stand waiting on the platform until the train left. The wait was long and unbearable. His big face was red from the effort of holding back the tears. We looked at each other in silence, as usual, but I realized that we were saying good-bye, and all I could do was pray for the train to leave and put an end to that heartrending look I'd never seen in his eyes before. There he stood on the platform, lower than me for the first time ever, so low that I could see how sparse his hair had become as he constantly turned his head to glance at the signal light at the end of the track. His big body was motionless, and he stood with his legs wide apart as if preparing to receive a blow, his hands like weights in the pockets of his overcoat, his eyes moist and his face red. And just as I was at last realizing that it meant something to be the only son, just as I was about to open my mouth and yell to him that I was getting off the train and that we would find a way to work things out without destroying our lives, the train gave a little lurch and began moving. And so, once again in silence, I was wrenched from him. I saw his big body give a start when the train moved. Then I saw him grow smaller the farther away I got. He didn't move, didn't make a gesture. Then he vanished from sight completely.

My period of respectability didn't last long. I was dismissed after a year, although, to be honest, it could have happened even earlier. The small Roman office was the last asset to be liquidated before the magazine closed down, along with the boom that had given birth to it. The place where I worked, drumming up a little advertising for the magazine and occasionally writing a few articles to indulge the medical profession's unfathomable fondness for literature, was a room filled with furniture upholstered in red damask in a neo-Renaissance villa just beyond the wall along the Tiber.

The owner was Count Giovanni Rubino di Sant'Elia, a distinguished man in his fifties with a nonchalant and somewhat affected manner. Distant at first, almost as if he came into my office only to open the French windows that looked out on the garden and allow me to breathe in the scent of his lilacs, he ended up spending more and more time in the armchair in front of my desk and engaging me in conversations that became more familiar in tone as his true financial situation was revealed. When he told me he was completely ruined, we decided we could be on a first-name basis.

He lived with his wife, a plump blonde, disorientated by her husband's straitened circumstances, in the back part of the house, opening the door only to the baker's boy, and ever since she'd opened up one day only to be confronted with some fellow who had then confiscated the magnificent gilded table in the drawing room, I'd been obliged to play the part of their somewhat bumbling secretary. But I was glad to do it. Especially for him. I liked seeing him come into my office, smooth the gray hairs at his temples with his hands, and jerk his elbows so that the cuffs of his spotless shirt shot out from the sleeves of his jacket. "So what are we doing, working?" he would say. Then I would put the cover on the typewriter and take out a bottle. He never talked, as a Milanese would have, about his financial problems, only about pleasant things—aristocrats and celebrities and, above all, women and horses—and sometimes telling quite risqué jokes with a gleam in his eye.

When summer arrived, we got in the habit of moving into the drawing room, and there, when the sun retreated from that part of the house, the two of us surrounded by walls that bore lighter patches where the furniture had been removed, the count would play his Steinway grand and I would sprawl on the last remaining couch and listen to him. And every afternoon, as soon as I heard those first notes, I would telephone a nearby bar, order some cold beer, and join him. There he would be, wearing an old silk dressing gown, hopelessly carried away. He would dredge up his repertoire, old songs I'd heard from my mother, tunes by Gershwin and Cole Porter, but, above all, an old American song called "Roberta." Sometimes, we would sing together.

On the first day of fall that year came the letter that shut the office. I informed the count, who leaned on the piano and smiled. "Well, my friend," he said, "what will you do now?" That's all he said, although I should have known that for him it was a fatal blow. Two days later, as I gathered my papers, there was a knock at the door, and four determined-looking workmen loaded the piano on their backs and took it away. It was quite an effort for them to get it through the gate, and the old Steinway must have hit some corner or other because its voice rose from the street in a kind of death knell. The whole time the operation lasted, the count didn't leave his room, but when I shook hands with the countess, who was visibly moved, and walked out of the house, I saw him at the window, raising his hand and waving to me. There was something so uncompromising in his gesture that I responded in the only way I thought appropriate: I put my bag down on the pavement and bowed.

For a few days after the office closed, I stayed in my hotel, pondering my future. The only thing the contacts I'd made through the magazine could offer me was a job in a pharmaceutical firm outside the city, where I would have to write advertising material from nine in the morning to six in the evening. I decided to wait for something to happen. Like an aristocrat under siege.

Every day I would go to the sea. With a book in my pocket, I would take the metro to Ostia and spend most of the day reading in a little trattoria on the beach. Then I would go back to the city and hang around the Piazza Navona area, where I'd made a few friends, all of them adrift like me, intellectuals, for the most part, with the anxious but expectant look of refugees. Rome was our city, she tolerated us, flattered us, and even I ended up realizing that in spite of the sporadic work, the weeks when I went hungry, the damp, dark hotel rooms with their yellowing furniture squeaking as if killed and desiccated by some obscure liver disease, I couldn't live anywhere else. And yet, when I think back on those years, I have clear memories of a small number of places, a small number of events, because Rome by her very nature has a particular intoxication that wipes out memory. She's not so much a city as a wild beast hidden in some secret part of you. There can be no half measures with her, either she's the love of your life or you have to leave her, because that's what the tender beast demands, to be loved. That's the only entrance toll you'll have to pay from wherever you've come, from the green, hilly roads of the south, or the straight, seesawing roads of the north, or the depths of your own soul. If she's loved, she'll give herself to you whichever way you want her, all you need to do is go with the flow and you'll be within reach of the happiness you deserve. You'll have summer evenings glittering with lights, vibrant spring mornings, café tablecloths ruffled by the wind like girls' skirts, keen winters, and endless autumns, when she'll seem vulnerable, sick, weary, swollen with shredded leaves that are silent underfoot. You'll have dazzling white steps, noisy fountains, ruined temples, and the nocturnal silence of the dispossessed, until time loses all meaning, apart from the banal aim of keeping the clock hands turning. In this way you too, waiting day after day, will become part of her. You too will nourish the city. Until one sunny day, sniffing the wind from the sea and looking up at the sky, you'll realize there's nothing left to wait for.

Every now and again, someone did get the hell out. When it was the turn of Glauco and Serena, two of the Piazza Navona group, I moved into their apartment on Monte Mario. By now I was at the end of my tether with hotel rooms, and I couldn't believe I was actually going to have a place I could call my own. When I also bought their worn-out Alfa Romeo for fifty thousand lire, I naturally thought I'd reached a significant turning point in my life. I packed two suitcases with my books and moved in the same day they left. They were going because Serena had managed to get a two-year contract as a set designer in a theater in Mexico City, but above all because their marriage was in trouble and Glauco had stopped painting. Rome had crushed them and they were leaving, taking their unlikely names and an excessive number of suitcases with them. "Lousy city," Glauco said, looking out from the balcony.

"I like it here."

"Really? Then why are you always drunk?"

"Not always," I said. "Often. There's a big difference." Then I looked at the valley stretching below. It was vast, cut in half by a multi-arch bridge crossed several times a day by a train as long and silent as a caterpillar. On either side rose the walls of two convents, alive with bells when the sun went down, while, opposite, the closest buildings merged with the greenery on the horizon. The sky was high and wide, and so was the light. It was a gorgeous spot.

"It's all yours," Glauco said, indicating the room we were in. No need to make an inventory: there was an old armchair, a bookcase, and a sofa bed. The other two rooms weren't furnished at any greater expense, pleasant, old furniture from the Porta Portese flea market, for the most part. One room was almost completely filled with canvases, cans of paint, and all the things a painter usually needs. "If you run out of money, don't sell the paintings," Glauco said, as if anyone might want to buy them. He went out, saying that he still had to say good-bye to someone in town. He didn't ask me to go with him, and I guessed that he was going to say good-bye to his girlfriend. Everyone knew he had another woman. A burly, aggressive type, he could never avoid boasting. He even knew there was a very definite fondness between Serena and me, but he left us alone because he wasn't the kind of man to fear anyone.

Serena was still in the bedroom, surrounded by open suit-cases. She must have been afraid they would swallow her, because she was walking up and down, wringing her hands. "Where's Glauco?" she said. I told her he'd be back soon, and she continued to move around the room with an air of tragedy. When she passed me for the third time, I finally put an arm around her shoulders, and she huddled against my chest and looked at me in confusion. But when I hugged her tighter, she stiffened, and I realized the answer was no, that she would have liked it to be yes, but some other time, right now it was no, it was too late. We talked about Mexico until Glauco came back.

"So," he said, "shall we go?" I was surprised by the sadness in his voice. That final farewell must have been particularly hard. Standing in the middle of the room, with that muscular body of his, he had the cheated, immature look of a heavyweight who's lost his title. For the first time, I felt a kind of fondness for him.

I went with them to the airport. We said good-bye, kissing one another's cheeks, and then I went up to the observation platform to watch them leave. As they climbed the steps up to the plane, they looked around for me. We waved at one another until they got on board. The plane took a while to get going, but at last it moved toward the center of the runway, where it stopped, as if to catch its breath, taxied, then started gathering speed until it rose out of sheer force of habit and kept climbing, glittering in the sun, and at last disappeared. Only then did I leave the airport.

On my way back to the city, I thought about other farewells. I thought about when I'd said good-bye to my father and when I'd said good-bye to Sant'Elia, and I thought about how all these farewells had changed my life. But it's always like that, we are what we are not because of the people we've met but because of those we've left. That's what I was thinking, as I calmly drove the old Alfa Romeo. It was as slow and noisy as a whale, and the birds in the trees fell silent as the car passed, as if a dark cloud had crossed the sky. It had a list of owners as long as the phone book of some provincial town, but its aroma of ash and leather was almost intoxicating.

I decided to make a serious attempt to stop drinking. I would sit out on the balcony in the sun, reading, and keep away from bars and the people who frequented them. The heat made the mixture of sweet wine and cold water I was using to wean myself off alcohol a little less disgusting, and gradually I even started to put on weight. The hardest part was the evenings, when I'd leave the copy department of the *Corriere dello Sport* and have to face those dead hours that stretch from ten o'clock to one in the morning. Girls were a great help to me. I'd always been lucky with girls, and in those months my battle with alcohol aroused their maternal instincts, so it often happened that I would wake up in strange beds, alone, since the girls I went out with were mostly teachers or salesclerks, which meant they had to keep regular hours. And it was great to wake up like that, truth be told. I'd get up, wander around the apartment, switch on the record player, check to see if coffee had been made and find it almost always had been, so that all I had to do was reheat it. Then I'd walk into clean bathrooms strewn with towels, brushes, hairpins, and mysterious jars of pale-colored creams. I'd look for an actual bathtub, almost always find it, and spend a long time soaking in it. Finally I would dry myself, get dressed, and leave, closing the door behind me and hearing the sound echo in the empty apartment.

Out on the street, I would buy a newspaper, glance at the secondhand books in the stalls, stock up on provisions, and go back home, trying to decide whether to spend the afternoon reading, at the movies, or at the newspaper office. It was on one of these mornings that I realized I didn't have any money in my pockets. It wasn't an unusual situation at all, but in this case it was complicated by a whole series of other misfortunes: the door I had irrevocably closed behind me, the car I had left the previous evening in a remote part of the city, the nagging feeling I'd forgotten something, something I couldn't remember however hard I tried. It looked like it was going to be one of those days when our shirt buttons come off in our hands, we lose our address book, we miss our appointments, and every door turns into a trap for our fingers. One of those days when the only thing to do is shut ourselves in and wait for it to pass. But I couldn't do that, so I set off on foot, in the rain.

Yes, apart from anything else, it was raining. I remember that day's rain very well. A spring rain falling intermittently on a forgetful, surprised city and filling it with scents that became ever more fragrant after every shower. So much so that there isn't another day in my life as rich in scents as the one on which this story began.

2

I got to Piazza del Popolo with an empty stomach and my shoes full of water. The square was overrun with parked cars, and a single beam of sunlight, high in the sky, made the terraces of the Pincio shimmer. The two cafés were full of people annoyed by the fact that they couldn't sit outside. Under the awning of Rosati's, I found chairs piled one on top of the other. I grabbed one and looked around for a friendly face, someone who might buy me lunch, but the only people I saw were people I couldn't stand. Then it started pouring again, so I headed for Signor Sandro's. He was an old barman, with measured, skillful moves, who'd opened an elegant watering hole with red leather chairs and prints on the walls. It was frequented mainly by literary types, poets, film-makers, and a few radical journalists, who ate steak and carrots, but naturally that day I couldn't find anybody I was friendly enough with to invite me to lunch. It was a place where I had credit, though, so I ordered a hamburger and a glass of Barolo and sat watching one of my favorite spectacles, Signor Sandro making cocktails. It was at the climax of this spectacle that a magnificent silk umbrella was lowered in the doorway and, too late to be of any use to me, Renzo Diacono appeared. I hadn't seen him for a while, not since he too had ended up working in television. "Leo!" he said loudly on seeing me. He was very well dressed, unlike the bearded giant he'd come in with, who immediately vanished in the crowd at the counter. "What are you drinking?" he said.

"Nothing."

"Nothing?" For a moment, he seemed about to say something, then, with his Piedmontese tact, he merely asked me when I might be available for a game of chess. "I don't have time for serious things anymore," he said, indicating his companion, who was returning from his siege of the bar. That was the great thing about him. Whoever he was with, he always gave the impression he'd rather be with you. "How's life?"

"I don't know," I said. "I can only answer for my own."

"Congratulations," the bearded giant said, joining us with his glass. "Very wise." He raised his glass to me. He was wearing a military greatcoat, with a scarf that went all the way down to his feet, and a streaming umbrella hanging from his arm, and was considering the world from the sublime heights of a massive hangover. He had a ravaged smile, the smile of a veteran. Renzo said he was the best director in television, when he was sober, but that was a condition he probably hadn't been in for some time now. Giggling, the man apologized, in reply to Renzo's remark, and went to get a refill.

"Why don't we get together this evening?" Renzo said. He also said that he and his wife had moved and made me repeat their new address twice to make sure I wouldn't forget it. But there was no danger of that. Even though we were a generation apart, I enjoyed his company, he was a good chess player as well as a highly regarded historian, and his wife, Viola, was an excellent cook. I couldn't ask for anything better to conclude such an unlucky day.

When I was alone again, I drew up a plan that would be proof against bad luck. First of all, I'd go to the newspaper office to wangle some money, then I'd catch a movie, then I'd proceed to the Diaconos'— having first gone to pick up my old Alfa Romeo. It was such a simple, such a reassuring plan that the combination of it and the wine gave me an immediate feeling of euphoria. I walked out and smelled the rain, which was coming to an end. Big, isolated drops were falling on the sidewalk, and there were large patches of blue in the sky. I set off past the damp but dazzling buildings of the Corso, and ten minutes later walked into the offices of the *Corriere dello Sport*, humming "Où es-tu, mon amour?" in the Django Reinhardt version.

The girls at the typewriters, with their headsets on, greeted me with little cries of surprise—this wasn't the time I usually showed up—and when I asked for Rosario, they pointed me to a booth, from which my friend emerged at that very moment, browner in the face than the wax disc he was holding. "Well, look who's here!" he said as he passed me. I didn't lose heart. Even though it was obvious there was no work for me, I could still ask for a loan. He knew that too, so he withdrew into his own headset and immediately set to work playing back the disc and typing out its contents. I sat down and looked at him until he had to give in. "How much do you want?" he said, putting his hand in his pocket. He gave me exactly half of what I asked him for, and on top of that I had to listen to a lecture. How much longer did I think I could continue like this? Didn't I know that the head of the department was tired of not being able to rely on me? The job was there, why didn't I take it? He'd gotten me the job, which entitled him to speak. He was a good friend, a melancholy southerner with a discontented wife. He'd left his village, on a promontory overlooking the blue Ionian Sea, to come to Rome and work as a journalist, but all he'd ended up doing was recording other people's articles onto wax discs, then transcribing them. The complete idiocy of the job was proving a discouraging end to the years of his youth, but he didn't give up. He was small and dark, weary but indomitable.

I got the hell out of there. Outside, it was pouring. Torrents of water hammered down on the decapitated statues of the Forum, the collapsed columns, the palaces in the paved squares, the desolate afternoon arenas, the ornate churches, and, absurdly, the overflowing fountains. For a while I waited in a doorway, splashed by rain and cursed at by passersby—other castaways seeking salvation, like me, in the dark, cavelike entrance— then, taking advantage of a break in the weather, I ran, hugging the walls, until I reached a small movie theater nearby. They were showing something with my poor sweetheart, Marilyn Monroe—I refused to think of her as dead—and I watched it all the way through twice, eating salted seeds and listening to the thunder rolling over the roofs of the houses. By the time I came out, I was madly in love with her and very badly disposed toward the world, because a dead sweetheart is already sad enough in and of itself without there having to be rain too.

There was something cruel about the evening. The crowd had come streaming back out onto the streets, but the traffic was un-naturally suspended, paralyzed. From time to time, the sizzling lights of streetcars illumined the rain-swollen sky. The newspaper headlines spoke of landslides, floods, delayed trains. To the north of the city, the river had overflowed its banks, spreading out into the fields, and the people waiting at the bus stops were staring up at the sky in silence. Glumly, I realized it was too late to try to recover the old Alfa Romeo, and I was forced to head immediately for the Diaconos'. I set off on foot, but soon enough had to take shelter in the entrance of a store that was still open. The traffic had drained away as if by magic, and the street was now deserted. Through the rain, I could hear a radio broadcasting the evening news. They were saying that the weather would change, that spring had arrived in our part of the world. It was at this point that a taxi appeared. I stopped it, told the driver where to go, sat down, and wrung out the cuffs of my trousers. Then I sat back and looked at the city until the meter warned me I couldn't spend any more.

*The wind was rising by the time I got to an apartment block sur-*rounded by a damp, rustling garden. It was only then, perhaps because of the smell of the wet earth, that it occurred to me I should have brought Viola some flowers, but it was too late now, and I was so hungry I could barely stand. So I kept on, confronting the final test, an elevator that throughout the ride up emitted a menacing drone, as if complaining about my weight. Reaching the third floor, I quickly tidied my hair and rang the doorbell. Viola appeared. She looked surprised. Before I could say anything, she let out a little hiccup and burst into irrepressible laughter. I must have looked like a flood victim to her. "Come in, Leo," she said, taking me by the arm. "God, how happy I am to see you. How did you manage to find us?"

Those were her exact words, and it only took Renzo leaping to his feet when I walked into the living room for me to realize he'd completely forgotten he'd invited me. "Leo!" he said loudly, for the second time that day. A dozen people turned their heads languidly to look at us. They were sunk in an equal number of armchairs strewn across the vast rugs of the room, and all of them had the satisfied look of people who'd already eaten. There were introductions, to which I responded through clenched teeth.

"You're soaked," Renzo said with guilty attentiveness. "Sit down by the fire. What can I get you?"

"A little bit of luck," I said. But he'd turned and was now pushing a cart in my direction. I hesitated. It had been a while since I'd last seen so many bottles in a place that wasn't a bar. I chose a scotch, and as Renzo's hand searched among the bottles they clinked triumphantly. For a while I was the center of attention, with Renzo telling the others how much his book about pirates owed to me. I'd always been very good at helping other people with their work, but Renzo praised me with such conviction, it was as if I'd written the book myself. I even had to answer a few questions on the subject before I was able to disappear into the armchair nearest the fireplace and practice the only two skills I'd ever really mastered: keeping quiet and adapting myself to my surroundings. My return to anonymity coincided with the discovery of a bowl filled with peanuts. Viola joined me. "Hey," she said, "you look like a monkey with his spoils." I put the bowl down on the rug and she sat down on the arm of my chair. I looked her over. In the two years since we'd last seen each other, her sweet face had become almost placid, but her legs were the same as ever, the most beautiful I'd ever seen. "Would you agree to be cryogenically frozen?"

"Only if I was in love."

"Oh, how cute!" She laughed. "I'm conducting a survey, and then I'll make my decision," she said apologetically. "And don't make fun of me. No, let's talk about us instead. Who goes first?" She made the gesture of someone cutting a deck of cards. "You," I said, to give myself time to recover and retreat into my own daydreams. I was an expert at this, truth be told. With just a few *of courses* and a few *maybes*, I was capable of making anyone feel I was listening to them with seriousness and understanding. That's what I did with her, actually taking advantage of the respite to try to fill in the blank that had been throbbing in my head since morning. I'd have given the whole bowl of peanuts to know what it was I'd forgotten to do that day, but I really couldn't remember, so I contented myself with the warmth of the flames under my wet shoes until the fire and the alcohol had on me too the comforting effect that makes them both indispensable at social gatherings, where you would never say out loud that the former might burn the building down and the latter might make you feel as if you're freezing to death on the sunniest morning of your life. ". . . I couldn't stand those converted bathrooms anymore," Viola said, apparently concluding a speech I hadn't heard.

"I imagine you must have a beautiful bathroom here," I said, remembering the lovely old apartment on Campo de' Fiori, where they'd lived before.

"Oh, it's palatial! You absolutely must see it!" For a moment, I thought she was going to take me by the hand and drag me there whether I liked it or not. "And what about you, are you still in that little hotel downtown?" But there was no need to answer, because just then a voice rose up from the armchairs, begging to begin a parlor game, and she had to leave me. Alone now, I started making an inventory of the people around me. For them, the rain was just a pretext to get dressed up in the right way—that much was clear from the start. With their velvet trousers, woolen shirts, and heavy shoes, they made it clear that, yes, of course they knew perfectly well how things were outside, in that world full of rain and sordidness, but they also knew that a glass of Chivas Regal and a pleasant chat with friends would allow them to ignore the multitudes pressing against the walls.

Some of us are besieged, others do the besieging, I was thinking by the time I was on my second drink, and those doing the besieging are weary with hunger and homesickness. That's what I was thinking, as my eyes kept wandering toward the huge white velvet couch on which a man and a girl sat with the absent demeanor of two birds at rest. The man, perched on the arm of the couch in a tangle that suggested he was uncommonly tall and from which his hands stuck out like two short, useless wings, made you think of a bird that, evolving over time, had somehow lost touch with the sky. As for the girl, she was very beautiful. On that couch, she indeed looked like a migratory bird that had found a boat in which to rest while waiting for a storm to pass. Absent, alien, vaguely nervous.

*I'd only just managed to get the bowl of peanuts back into my posses-*sion when Renzo took me by the arm and forced me to let go of it and follow him between the armchairs. "What are they promising you now?" he said, referring to the left-wing newspapers for which he'd worked before getting into TV.

"I don't know, I don't know anything about promises," I said pointedly, but he was too caught up in what he was saying to grasp that I was alluding to his having forgotten his invitation to me.

"A job in television, that's what they're promising you, certainly not the revolution. Well, all I did was get in ahead of the rest." He waited for a sign of approval from me. I gave it to him. "When you feel like a job in television," he went on, "all you have to do is ask for it. You have no idea what a bunch of idiots everyone there is. As long as you're not an idiot, they'll think you're a genius."

"But of course!" a woman huddled deep in an armchair said with embarrassing swiftness. She had been listening to the same record since I came in. "This friend of yours," she said, looking at me, "doesn't look much like a pirate. If anything, he could be one of those stowaways in Conrad. You know, one of those men who've committed some terrible sin and expiate it by wandering from port to port? God, how I love him!"

"Who, him?" Renzo said, pointing at me.

"Conrad," the woman said. The record had come to a close,

and she put the needle back at the beginning. I wondered which of the two would win in the end. She again gave it her full attention. There was no trace of sorrow in her, or of passion. Her whole demeanor exuded independence, an independence so absolute as to make you think she hadn't come into the world like everybody else, in pain and blood, but had simply emerged, like a butterfly.

"Eva, you'll get appendicitis if you just sit there all the time," Viola said, joining us before my silence could grow too heavy. Renzo took the opportunity to lead me away, and once again he did so by taking my arm, as if the room was as big as a public square. It was, in fact, big, but not quite as big as his gesture seemed to suggest. After a few steps, we almost bumped into the companion of the girl. He was wandering through the living room with the air of having just hit a piece of furniture in a spontaneous attempt to take flight. She was alone now, on the white velvet couch. With her fingers twined in her long black hair, she was nervously laying out a deck of cards for a game of solitaire as if some redemptive response might come from it. Renzo pulled the bar cart over to her. He'd noticed the direction of my glances and with his usual discretion was taking care of things. "What are you drinking, Arianna?"

She took her eyes away from her own destiny. "Anything above forty proof," she said. From the smile she gave me, anybody would have thought she'd spent the whole evening waiting for me. It was a smile that isolated the person it was addressed to, raising him to heights he would never have suspected he could conquer. A smile like a blow to the head, in which only one thing remained unequivocal. That she didn't give a damn about you. "What about that game?" she said, as if the progress of the evening depended on me. I spread my palms wide.

"Here it is!" Viola said, joining us with paper and pencil. Then she took me by the arm and said, "Come with me. You're not thinking of betraying me with some nymphet!" So I had to go back to my armchair, where I discovered that the bowl of peanuts had disappeared. Ten minutes later, in the silence of the living room, the only sound was the scratch of pencils on paper, the occasional laugh, and, I feared, the rumbling of my stomach.

It was at this point that another soft noise pervaded the room. The girl, Arianna, had abandoned her couch and was proceeding miraculously between the armchairs. The fragility of her body made whatever she did seem courageous, even just walking across a room full of friends. With every step, her glossy rain boots emitted little sighs around her knees. She reached the arm of Viola's chair and leaned down to whisper something in her ear.

It was now that the woman named Eva intervened, saying, "Come on, Arianna, stop it!" Then, to Viola: "Don't you think she's dumb? This morning as she was putting on her blouse, she scratched a spot on her skin, and all day long she's been trying to phone Venice to talk to her doctor about it."

The girl barely looked at her, then said she'd heard of people who'd *died* from scratching a mole.

"Really, Arianna?" Viola said. "Do you have a consultant you trust?"

Well, that's how things were. The girl had gone to make her phone call, and I was trying to find an excuse to leave and go somewhere to eat when Viola, seeing that I couldn't make up my mind to write my anonymous message on the sheet of paper, looked at me pensively and said, "Listen, would you go get the ice from the kitchen? I'm sorry, but Ernesto isn't here, it's his night off." Because now they even had a servant. She gave me directions on how to get to the kitchen, informing me that I would find it changed and that only the refrigerator was still the old one.

I had a flash of hope. Two years earlier, that refrigerator had been the best stocked in the city. "My old friend!" I said. "How is he?"

"Oh, you know," she said. "One of those cold, unsatisfied types. An aesthete."

I was already on my feet. In the hallway, the girl was phoning, curled up on the floor, in the dark. I had to climb over her and then went on my way, sensing her eyes on my back as I groped along the wall in search of the kitchen door and the light switch. The light came on to reveal a kitchen as dazzlingly white as an operating room. The refrigerator was in a corner, a bit yellow compared with the rest of the furniture. With the flaking on its door looking like decoration, it stood there, lordly and reserved, but I wasn't intimidated, and, after searching in the pantry for bread, I walked resolutely over to it. The door opened with a slight click.

Inside, it was full of cool air and French cheeses. Holding the door open with one knee, I ate half a Camembert without any qualms, then, using a knife, levered under the ice tray until that frozen heart of aluminum came loose with a crack so tragic as to make me fear I'd murdered not only the refrigerator but the whole kitchen. Still eating, I turned on the faucet and let hot water run on the tray until the ice broke up, then emptied the cubes into the bucket and went back to the refrigerator. The still-open door lent it a violated air. I looked in the vegetable compartment until I found a very green and velvety zucchini. I placed it on the open wound left by the ice tray and closed the door with the appropriate care. It wouldn't be the first aesthete to have a zucchini in place of a heart, and, anyway, it was the nearest thing to a flower that I had at hand.

The girl was still in the dark on the floor, and I was about to climb over her again when I felt her grab me by the jacket. It was an imperious gesture to the point that, almost without realizing it, I found myself kneeling next to her, with the ice bucket in my hand. I was surprised to see that she was crying. I tried to think of something to say to her, but I couldn't think of anything, so I simply stayed there, by her side, while an ironic but consoling voice on the phone kept telling her that she wouldn't die. The girl didn't say anything. All she did was listen and cry, and then, when the voice stopped, she stood up, passed the back of her hand over her nose, and vanished in the direction of Viola's bathroom, leaving me to replace the receiver. I didn't take it amiss. I knew the type. There are people who have the singular characteristic of asking for help while at the same time giving you the impression they're doing you a favor. I put back the telephone and returned to the living room with the ice bucket. Immediately afterward, I began shivering. I knew what it was. One of the most unpleasant effects of alcohol was that it screwed up the part of my brain that regulated my body heat. I went and smoked a cigarette next to what remained of the fire, and soon after that the girl returned. Her transformation was amazing. Nobody could have suspected that, only a short while earlier, tears had been streaking down her conceited face. The perfunctory glance she gave me made me feel I was no more to her than a handkerchief.

The party came to an end about three. The guests abandoned their armchairs and left, as if answering a call. Everything happened so quickly, I had the impression after a while that I was watching a movie whose projectionist has started showing the remaining footage at double the speed. But that, too, might have been an effect of the alcohol, I don't know. All I do know is, within a quarter of an hour the room was silent. A curtain swayed in front of an open window, and the turntable was going around and around beneath a pile of empty glasses and full ashtrays.

Viola and the girl were plotting on the couch, Renzo was sucking at an empty pipe, absorbed in his own thoughts, and I was looking at the titles of the books on a shelf. When I moved on to the paintings hanging on the walls, one of them, a freight car abandoned on a disused line, reminded me of my old Alfa Romeo abandoned on the other side of the city.

"You stay here," Viola said to Renzo, who was about to get up from his armchair. "He can see Arianna home. I've been trying to throw them into each other's arms all evening, and now you want to ruin everything?"

Without saying a word, the girl started collecting her cards, then walked out to the entryway, and Viola took the opportunity to throw me a knowing glance. A moment later, the girl reappeared, wearing a red plastic raincoat that made a loud rustling noise. She put the pack of cards in her pocket. "I'm ready," she said as if a firing squad awaited her outside. At the door, there were the usual promises of telephone calls and even an official invitation to dinner. In the old days, I would merely have had to turn up at the right time without even calling ahead.

"You'll have to go down on foot," Viola said. "Arianna hates elevators."

The girl didn't say a thing. We descended the stairs in silence, making sure we waited for each other at each landing.

Outside, the air was shaken by faint gusts of wind. Winter and spring were exchanging their last blows. The seasons change at night, unbeknown to the people, and we were witnessing a spectacle whose grandeur was only equaled by the silence with which it crept up on us. It was one of those nights when you feel that anything might happen. Next to me, the girl, remote, her hands clasped over her raincoat, her eyes half closed, was greedily breathing in the scent of the plane trees with the satisfaction of someone finding herself in her own garden together with a chance guest. To regain a little composure, I looked up at the sky.

It was black and very high, interspersed with big, racing clouds.

3

By the time we got in the car, the street-corner clocks said it was three in the morning. The city was drying out in the night wind, but there were still puddles as big as lakes, and the little English car swished past them. The girl drove in silence, proud of her profile, and I was already thinking that I would soon exit her life—as I would the life of any bus driver, with the door slamming behind me and the driver watching me in the rearview mirror—when she shook out her hair, and said, "What was your name again?"

"Leo Gazzara," I said. "It still is."

"What a sad name," she said after a while. "It sounds like a lost battle." After the day I'd had, I didn't feel up to rebutting that, so all I did was search my pockets for a cigarette. As always at that hour of the night, I was betrayed by the fluid in my lighter. I struck it a few times without success. She told me to have a look on the backseat, where I found a few cheap cigarettes, a copy of *Swann's Way*, and a bottle of French perfume.

"*Coeur Joyeux*," I read on the label. "You mean, not only do you have a heart, it's actually joyful?"

There was something grateful about her laugh. "It's my anti-dote," she said. "Do you live with someone, or what?"

"Or what," I said.

"Do you always talk this way?" she said.

We had reached the avenue where I'd left the old Alfa Romeo, so I didn't reply. Nobody had stolen it and it was grazing in soli-tude. "This is it," I said. "Thanks for the ride."

"You're welcome," she said. "And I'm sorry about that scene in the hallway. I'm hysterical tonight."

She'd finally said it.

"Why?"

"Oh, no reason," she said, switching off the engine. A glassy silence fell over the avenue. Around us, the buildings seemed to huddle over the sidewalks, and although the sky was still uni-formly black, there was a sense that night was slowly orienting itself toward dawn—it's from three o'clock onward that night rises from its own abyss, dripping with dreams. Any night watch-man can tell you that. "Want one?" she said, holding out a pack of very strong French cigarettes. "They'd kill a running buffalo."

"No," I said, "I've already had a weird enough day."

"Don't talk to me about weird days," she said. "Are you sleepy?"

I was at the end of my tether, truth be told. "Not so much," I said.

"I'm not sleepy at all," she said. She was silent for a moment, then threw me a hesitant glance. "Are you ever scared you'll forget to breathe while you're asleep?" That's what she said, and when I started laughing she looked embarrassed.

"Well," I said, "bars are good places when you're scared. I know one that's open all night, although the clientele's a bit dubious."

"You know," she said, starting the car again as if she hadn't expected anything else, "my demands are few when it gets to this time of night!"

"Are you referring to me?"

"No," she said, with a smile, "you're nice. Where are you from? Everyone in Rome is from somewhere else, have you noticed that?" Her change in mood was startling. She was almost expansive now. "What a horrible city!" she said when I mentioned Milan, then, fearing she'd upset me, said the streetcars there were great, and every time she visited she always took a ride on one.

She was from Venice, as I knew, from San Rocco to be precise, which made me think of Tintoretto's *Crucifixion*, and the struggle a painter with that diminutive name must have had to produce such a big picture. I asked her why she'd left.

"*Why?* Don't you read the papers?"

"You mean they mentioned your leaving?" I said.

She laughed. "Oh, only the local ones! They even brought out a memorial edition! No, I meant because of the sea. It's terrible, knowing you're sinking into the sea." I looked at her. I liked looking at her. Her eyes were too big and her mouth too determined, but all things considered it was they, her eyes and her mouth, that declared courage to still be the ultimate human resource.

"*Look, it's yellow!*" she said loudly, seeing a car pass. She knew a game, a kind of solitaire without cards, that could begin only when you saw a yellow car in motion. When it passed, you needed to make a wish and keep your fist clenched until you saw washing hung out to dry, a young man with a beard, a dog with a short tail, and an old man with a stick. It sounded like something that would never end.

"Listen," I said, "that sounds like it'd never end. Wouldn't it be better to stop for a drink and then go home?"

"I get it," she said. "You're just like all the others. Oh God! Why do people always live as if life can be repeated?"

At this point all I could do was keep quiet if I didn't want to come across like some office clerk, so I kept quiet as we drove into a service station on Via Flaminia. A few slow, powerful trucks passed us, creating an earthquake, before vanishing northward into the dark. Arianna pressed her clenched fist on the horn. After a few minutes, a guy dressed in yellow came out of the booth and walked over to us, rubbing his face with his hand. "Were you asleep?" she said, with mock innocence.

"No," he said, "I was fishing."

But Arianna wouldn't be put off and gave him one of her radiant smiles, as if she were ecstatic that he was the one who would be serving her. The guy was so invigorated by this, he even cleaned the windows without being asked.

"All right," she said, setting off again. "But first I want to eat. What would you say to a warm brioche?"

"I'd say I'd like a dozen of them," I said.

She knew the night like the back of her hand. A quarter of an hour later, we were pushing open the door of a bakery tucked away in a courtyard near the Palace of Justice, and entering a white hell of flour and people at work. There were men taking flaccid masses of dough and pounding them on the tables as if to punish them for their submissiveness, and others cutting them into pieces and sticking them in an oven. There were also women with white kerchiefs over their hair, mixing cream in containers.

"Oh, it's you, princess," one of them said. "What do you want tonight?"

Arianna pointed to various types of brioche while the women looked on indulgently. A paper cone was filled for her. She took it in both hands, because it was warm and pleasant to the touch, but that didn't stop her from stealing a madeleine, then nudging me with her elbow as I wished the women good night on the way out.

"What are you talking about, good night?" she said, once we were out in the courtyard. "These people have been working for hours!" She sighed. "I always feel really guilty coming here, but at this time of night I'd do anything for a warm brioche, wouldn't you?"

They were warm and fragrant, nothing like the sad little cakes you get in cafés, the ones the rest of the city would be dunking in their white-collar cappuccinos in a few hours' time. "There must be some advantage in being rich," I said, but she was miles away, swaying meditatively on the cobblestones of the courtyard in time to her chewing of the madeleine. "Are you looking for a loose paving stone?" I asked.

My display of Proustian culture impressed her. "There'd be no point," she said, looking at me, her curiosity aroused. "Madeleines aren't the way they used to be."

"Nothing's the way it used to be."

"That's a good beginning," she said. "Go on."

"Well," I said, "that's it, really. We're living in quite depressing times, but what can we do about it? We have no choice."

"No," she said, holding back a smile, "no choice at all. Have you ever thought how many pleasures progress has deprived us of?"

"Oh, sure. Drinking milk from glass bottles, for instance."

"Yes," she said. "That's not bad. What else?"

My suggestion was leafing through books without having to take off the plastic wrapper, to which she proposed blowing up paper bags, and I said slicing ham by hand, and she said walking on rubber soles and breaking glass decorations on the Christmas tree. When I stumped her with the smell of old leather armchairs, she changed the subject.

"When would you have liked to have been born?"

"In Vienna before the end of the empire," I said.

"Quite good," she said, getting in the car. "Me, in Combray. Do you mind driving? I'd like to see the city from the terraces of the Capitoline Hill."

We got there in five minutes and went and leaned on the

parapet just above the Forum. Beneath us, the squares were deserted, and the basilicas, frozen in marble, were dreaming of the day they would thaw.

"It's stupid," she said softly.

"What is?"

"Feeling nostalgic for something we never had." She turned to look at a few tramps sleeping on the benches. It wasn't too hard to find a young one with a beard for her game. "Basically, I envy them," she said. "They're so naturally part of things. What about you, what do you do for a living?" That wasn't an easy question to answer, so I told her I did nothing. "What do you mean, nothing?" she said. "Everyone does something. Even me, though it may not look like it. I'm studying architecture, I just haven't taken my exams yet. How do you spend your days?"

"Reading."

"And what do you read?"

"Everything."

"What do you mean, everything? Even streetcar tickets, labels on mineral water bottles, orders from the mayor for clearing snow?" She laughed.

"Yes, but I have a predilection for love stories," I said. She took me seriously and said she found them frustrating because for her to like them they had to end badly, and if they ended badly, she didn't like them. Had I read *À la recherche*? "I don't have enough breath in me," I said, maintaining that Proust was one of those writers who ought to be read aloud. The idea amused her, and she wanted to know which others that applied to. I mentioned the first books that came into my head: the Bible, *Moby-Dick*, the *Arabian Nights*. It struck me as a sufficiently *engagé* choice.

"You must have some favorites, though."

"Yes," I said. "Henry James Joyce, Bob Dylan Thomas, Scotch Fitzgerald, secondhand books in general."

"Why secondhand?" she said, not picking up on my erudite wordplay.

"Because they cost less and because you can tell in advance, with a fair amount of certainty, if they're worth reading."

"How so?" she said, sitting on the parapet.

So I told her I looked for bread crumbs or pieces of crust between the pages, because a book you read while nibbling your food was sure to be good, or else I looked for grease stains, fingerprints, and not too many pages with folded-down corners. "Where you should look for folding is at the spine. If you fold a book back at the spine when you're reading it, that means it's good. If it's a hardback, I look for stains, grazes, scratches—they're all reliable signs."

"What about if the person who read it before you was an idiot?"

"You have to know something about the author," I said. But in any case, I went on, evidence suggested that since the advent of television, reading had become such an outmoded activity as to endure only among people with a certain level of intelligence. "Readers are a dying species," I said. "Like whales, partridges, wild animals in general. Borges calls them black swans, and maintains that good readers are now scarcer than good writers. He says reading is an activity subsequent to writing, more resigned, more civil, more intellectual. No," I went on, "that's not where the danger lies. Books make different impressions according to the state of mind you read them in. A book that struck you as banal on a first reading may dazzle you on a second simply because in the meantime you suffered some kind of heartbreak, or you took a journey, or you fell in love. In other words, something happened to you."

So now she knew what kind of pretentious snob she was dealing with. She'd listened to me in silence, keeping her gaze fixed on the damp gravel of the garden. She looked up. "You're funny, you know," she said. "You looked *so tragic* when you showed up at Viola's."

"It was just hunger."

"Hunger?"

"Yes, ever hear of it?"

"Of course," she said, laughing, as we walked back to the car. "Isn't it that *Indian* thing you get when you have an aperitif?" Reaching the car, she sat down on the trunk and looked around. "It'd be fun to live here," she said, "but I don't feel like marrying the mayor."

"Where do you live?"

"Via dei Glicini," she said, her face lighting up. "Know where that is?"

"Over toward Viale dei Platani."

"Yes, and there's a street nearby called Via dei Lillà, which I like a lot, and there's also a Via delle Orchidee," she said, uttering the names of these flowers—wisteria, lilac, orchid—as if the streets were paved with them. "Drive me home," she said, letting me take the wheel.

"Please don't joke," I said, because if there was a place where someone like her couldn't possibly be living, that was the place. Instead of answering, she propped her boots on the dashboard.

I was at the end of my tether, as far as energy went, but I still wanted to know what she had in mind, so I headed in the direction of the infamous Via dei Glicini. It was a neighborhood I couldn't stand, a district of ramshackle streets crisscrossed by the most fucked-up streetcars I'd ever seen. The jerry-built houses were falling to pieces, and the sidewalks were lined with disgusting restaurants alternating with electrical appliance stores and auto body shops. Gangs of boys astride lethal motorbikes gunned their engines, making an infernal noise. A stench of disinfectant that knocked you back spewed out onto the sidewalks from the movie theaters, and in all of it there wasn't a single garden, a single tree, a single flowerbed to protect the inhabitants from the incessant summer sun, so that in the end the names of flowers on the street-corner signs made you feel as if you were in a madman's dream. What was someone like her doing in a place like this? Without saying another word, I plunged into the long, straight streets of the neighborhood, with their dim fluorescent lights. Huge human hives rose in the night on either side, like towering cemeteries. Arianna looked at them in silence, with those eyes of hers that were too big.

Once we'd passed a run-down amusement park and the perimeter wall of a vocational school, the car began to be reflected in the windows of the electrical goods stores. We wandered in the livid air until I found Via dei Glicini. It was a tunnel through lines of washing—at least that was one objective we'd reached in the game. Apart from that, it was just decay and squalor. "What are we doing here?" she said. "You got it all wrong, this isn't *my* Via dei Glicini."

"There aren't any others."

"Of course there are," she said. Then she grabbed the bottle of perfume and dabbed her wrists and temples. The smell of lilacs that pervaded the car did actually make the view of the street more bearable. A night watchman, dressed in black, was coming toward us, pushing his bicycle.

"Let's get out of here, please, I beg you!" she said with a moan. "Night watchmen give me the creeps."

She grabbed my hand and squeezed it hard until we were out of the neighborhood. The fact was, not only did she not live on Via dei Glicini, she'd never even been there, she said. That morning she'd read an ad about two rooms for rent, and the fact that the streets had the names of flowers made her think it was a nice residential area. On a map of the city, she'd seen it was more of an outlying district, but how could she ever have imagined it was such a *horrible* place? How *unlucky* she was! I didn't say a word. She must have been relying heavily on those flower names. What I really wondered was who she was running away from, because there was no doubt about it, she was trying to get the hell out, to escape. I wondered who from. Then I found out it was her sister. They'd quarreled that morning and Arianna had decided to leave home even though she was genuinely *terrified* of living alone. Had she really left with only the Proust book, a few matches, and a bottle of perfume? "And a deck of cards," she said, in that conceited way of hers. "Why not?" She never went anywhere without a deck, but, as for anything else, in the heat of the quarrel she'd forgotten her keys and locked herself out. That was something I could relate to. I thought about my own dumb departure in the rain that morning and all of a sudden I remembered what it was I'd forgotten. That was it! I'd spent my whole birthday trying to remember that it was my birthday.

"What? You *forgot*?"

"Well," I said, "birthdays aren't what they used to be." But I was thinking of all the things I'd intended to do, starting that day. Then I looked up at the sky, because apparently you always look up at the sky when you turn thirty.

"You must be crazy," Arianna said. "How can anyone forget their own birthday? I start crossing off the days on the calendar a month before!" Faced with such an extraordinary phenomenon, she'd forgotten all about Via dei Glicini and the rest of it. "We have to celebrate anyway," she said. "Let's find somewhere we can get a drink."

And that's what we did, as dawn came up over the city. In the gray air, groups of people were waiting for the first buses. It was the hour when anyone who's been on his feet all night demands something hot in his stomach, the hour when hands search for each other under the sheets as dreams become more vivid, the hour when the newspapers smell of ink and the first sounds of day start to creep out like an advance guard. It was dawn, and all that remained of the night were two shadows under the eyes of this strange girl by my side.

"*To all the things we haven't done, the things we should have done, and the things we won't do,*" I said, raising a cup of boiling hot caffè latte. Arianna laughed, said it seemed rather too *programmatic* a toast, but, basically, it was fine. Then she leaned across the table and gave me a kiss on the cheek. "And now," she said, settling back on the metal chair, "tell me something amusing." We were in a café at the bus terminal. Around us was the good smell of coffee, that good smell cafés have early in the morning, and a boy was spreading sawdust on the floor between the feet of a few drivers reading the *Corriere dello Sport*. I felt good after the coffee, even though my bones ached. So I told her my story about Via dei Glicini, where for a while I'd given Italian lessons to a gang of kids more ready to bum cigarettes off me than to consider Manzoni's *The Betrothed* anything other than an endlessly delayed fuck. During the last lesson, I should have been explaining the subjunctive, but I had a three-day hangover and couldn't keep still on my chair. They noticed, and started patting me on the back, which I pretended to enjoy in order to save face. In the end I couldn't hold out any longer and crashed to the floor. I think the father of one of my disciples took me back to my hotel on his motorbike, with me lying across it like a dead Indian, I don't really know. What I do know is, I wasn't paid even for the lessons I'd given when I was sober, and for a long time I planned to abduct one of the kids and demand ransom. Arianna was laughing, then stopped suddenly and sat looking at me over the rim of her cup. She was looking at me very closely, her eyes half shut.

"What's up?" I said.

"Nothing," she said. "I like your gray eyes. I was asking myself if I could fall in love with you."

"There's no need," I said, lighting a cigarette. "You can come to my place anyway, and stay as long as you like."

"Do you mean that?" she said. The idea excited her, and she immediately said she wouldn't be the least trouble, we could share the rent because she had an annuity of fifty thousand lire, which was at least something, and she knew how to cook a fabulous chateaubriand. At this point I felt like showing off a little, and I said she shouldn't make anything because it made me really sad to think of a poet who went down in history because of a steak. So she asked if I minded in the same way when it came to politicians, and we settled on Bismarck.

Then she started planning out our days. We would listen to music, read, and study, because she really had to resume her studies, get that damned degree, and go back to Venice, where she would be part of a team of technicians working to save the city. Except she could never really study properly, she was so disorganized, *so disorganized*!

"What time is it?" she asked, even though she had a heavy man's watch on her wrist. "This thing? Oh, it's a family heirloom." It wasn't accurate, and she'd never had it fixed, because, that way, looking at it was always a surprise. It was six o'clock, and the watch said a quarter to eight, though who knew what day?

"I'll be back," she said, getting up and going to the toilet. It was locked, and she had to ask the barista for the key. When she came back, she had a look of disgust on her face. "Maybe they keep it locked because they're afraid someone will go in and clean it," she said. "What shall we do?"

"We're going home, aren't we?" I said, managing to pry myself out of my chair, but Arianna shook her head. After a night spent smoking, the best thing was to run down to the sea and get some oxygen in our lungs, didn't I agree? I wondered if there was anything in the world capable of destroying her, fragile as she was.

She sat down behind the wheel, and ten minutes later we were zooming along the straight road leading to the coast, between meadows covered with dew and pines silhouetted blackly against the clear sky, which now had some color. Arianna kept talking in a slightly frenzied way, about the days we would spend together, and I shut my eyes to blot out the light and listened to the sound of her voice, thinking about how it would echo in the bare apartment facing the valley. God, there was still something that could be saved in this world!

The sea appeared suddenly at the end of the road. We started to drive alongside it as it appeared and disappeared between the beachside resorts. To our left, the out-of-season boardinghouses and hotels exposed their faded signs to a cool, tense wind that made the palms in their gardens sway.

Everything was very silent, even Arianna now. Once past the developed area, we parked on the side of the road. The sky was turning pink, but the sea was still gray and hostile.

"It always seems to be asking something," Arianna said after a while. "But all water's like that. The rain's the same, it always seems to be asking something."

When we walked down to the beach, the wind got in under our clothes and dispelled what little heat we'd accumulated in the car. She shivered. "It's cold, dammit," she said, and started running across the moist sand with her hands in the pockets of her red raincoat. In an instant she was far away, while I kept to the part of the beach that had hardened again, walking over a sad carpet of dried-out seaweed and empty shells. The waves lapped at my shoes, and gradually, as the undertow beat on the shore, a final barrier came down and my eyes moved to where her raincoat stood out like a red puppet. The noise it made, carried to me on the wind, was like the crinkling of a paper cone. I followed her tracks, placing my feet where she'd set hers. The wind played a strange trick when I reached her, making it look, as she turned her beautiful face toward me, wounded by the morning, as if she'd stopped breathing, then started again. The red raincoat emitted a few more squeals as her arms rose to my neck. I felt the cold of the sleeves on me and suddenly started to shiver again.

"Are you cold?" she said, pressing her body, small and hard and warm, against mine. She blew into the collar of my shirt, laughing softly, then I started to feel her lips running lightly over my cheeks. "Poor boy . . . poor boy . . . poor boy," she said softly, taunting me, "what have I done to you . . . you poor boy . . ." until I felt her lips gradually turning more tender as her smile faded. Her lips were on mine, and then I felt her tongue searching, tenderly, stubbornly, over my teeth, prying them apart. Then, with inexpressible slowness, she broke away and, still very slowly and thoughtfully, rubbed her lips on the cuff of my raincoat. "Well!" she laughed. "You won't even want to make love. I don't really like *that idea of yours.*"

She walked away, leaving me alone with my embarrassment. She joined a little group of fishermen dragging a net to shore. Part of it was still in the water, but it was already obvious that it hadn't been much of a catch, and the fishermen were cursing quietly among themselves as the sky turned from pink to blue.

"Look!" Arianna cried. "Please!"

And then I saw the magic transforming the morning. An old man was walking on the beach, risking a fall every time he raised his stick to urge on a filthy, aggressive dog with a docked tail.

Arianna opened her fist. She'd kept it shut for four hours.

"Ridiculous," I said, and with a clumsiness that even now torments me I tried to grab her hand, but she stuck it in the pocket of her raincoat.

By now the skyscrapers of EUR were gleaming in the sun. Arianna shook her hair out impatiently and lowered the sun visor on her side of the car. "Damn," she said. "I should have worn a pair of dark glasses. Why do I always make the wrong choices? I was so happy at the idea of going to your place, and now I have to go back to Eva!"

That's what she said, surprising me one last time. So Eva was the sister she was running away from. But in what way was it running away from someone if you spent the evening with them? She said they hadn't spent the evening together at all. They hadn't said a single word to each other all evening, hadn't I noticed?

I didn't say anything. I was very tired and couldn't stop shivering. I was at the end of my tether, and all I wanted now was my bed in my room overlooking the valley. Besides, if a day is the time separating the moment you get up from the moment you go back to bed, all I had to do to put an end to this day was to go to bed. Because it had been a god-awful day, truth be told.

"Shall I take you back to your car?" she said when we were back downtown.

A low, piercing sun shot out from above the roofs, splintering on the windows of the buildings, on the fountains, and on the sheet-metal surfaces of the cars. The streets were dry and here and there vast patches of dust indicated where the puddles had been.

"No, thanks," I said.

We'd reached the slopes of Monte Mario and stopped to give way to a line of men leaving a market. They looked stupid, carrying big bunches of flowers.

"But call me," she said when we were outside my building.

I looked at her. She was so beautiful it hurt. "Of course," I said.

Then I got out of the car and crossed the courtyard, once again feeling, as I had in the corridor at the Diaconos', her eyes on my back, like a weight. I stopped by the front door and listened to the car driving away. It disappeared, leaving an unbearable silence behind.

"Good morning, Signor Gazzara," the doorman said.

I said something in reply and started climbing the stairs, my legs shaking. The steps seemed higher than usual and I stumbled a couple times. This reminded me of occasions when I'd climbed the narrow stairs of hotels where I'd been living, mornings when I'd been hungover and confused. Just like then, the first thing I did when I got inside was look for a little bit of warmth. I crossed the apartment, which smelled of cigarette smoke and mustiness, and, in the uncertain light filtering through the shutters, went to the kitchen and took out my wonderful Ballantine's bottle, with its heraldic label, which I reserved for whenever I caught a chill. I filled it with boiling water, then took two aspirins and collapsed on the bed, clutching it to my stomach.

But the chill didn't go away. And so I did a stupid thing. I started crying.

4

I got out of bed four days later and, sneezing fiercely, caught a bus and went and recovered my old Alfa Romeo, feeling as if it was part of me that had been blown off in an explosion. On the way back, I stopped to buy more aspirin and a few provisions, then shut myself in at home, determined not to go out until the world had apologized to me.

It did its best, truth be told. The days were warm and the sky a disarming blue, but in a way the very beauty of the weather merely increased my anguish. I roamed the apartment, gripped by an invincible sense of futility. Even when I went out on the balcony to read and have a smoke, I caught myself wondering why I was doing it. I would go downstairs just to pick up my mail without any idea of what awaited me apart from the usual advertising flyers—for detergents, mainly—which I stuck in the mailbox next to mine. One time, I received a postcard from Graziano Castelvecchio. He was on Crete, and wrote: *There are stones here, don't come.* Another time, I found a letter from my family that I'd have preferred not to receive, all things considered, not so much because my mother was complaining that she hadn't seen me for a year but because my father was sending me money for me to buy him a set of Vatican stamps, which meant getting up at dawn and standing in line outside His Holiness's post office.

But there was so little I could do for him these days that the following morning there I was, yawning so much I almost fainted, standing with that little crowd of peaceful maniacs known as stamp collectors. Around ten, after I'd sent the stamps by registered mail, the beauty of the morning induced me to go read by the river. The area was deserted and I sat down on a deck chair with the book on my lap, but I couldn't concentrate and in the end I closed the book and sat there listening to the soft murmur of the traffic as it rolled across the bridges and watching the rowers gliding over the surface of the water like large dragonflies. Around two, I started to feel hungry and went to Signor Sandro's. The first person I saw was Annamaria. "Look at you!" she said on spotting me.

I hadn't seen her since she'd been fired by the paper she was working for because in an item on the funeral of a local dignitary she'd included the dead man's name among the names of the mourners. "What are you doing so far from home?" I said.

"I live around here now," she said, "on Via Whatsit, Via . . ." There were times she gave the impression she could hardly even remember her own name, but we'd spent some great evenings together.

"What are you doing this evening?"

"No idea. Ever since I went on a diet, I've been a hit with men."

"Only with men?" I said, remembering a fling she'd had with a very well-known theater actress.

She laughed. "What about you and girls, huh?" she said.

The pain I carried with me in my chest started to throb. So I made up my mind, asked for a telephone token, and went to make a call. The male voice that answered was very polite, and when I asked for the signora he hesitated in a professional manner. Soon afterward, I heard Viola's voice. "This is Leo," I said, and she gave one of her little laughs. "Stop laughing every time I get in touch."

"I laugh when I feel like it," she said. "Are we allowed to know where you've been? I've been trying to find you at that damned newspaper of yours for a week now. Don't you ever work?"

"Sick," I said. "I've been sick."

"I don't want to know about your problems. I want you to come over here today and keep me company. We'll have tea and I'll shorten some old skirts."

Basically, it was what I'd wanted, and so at five o'clock, the very hour when the marquise orders her carriage and goes out, I went to see her.

She was sitting by the window, with the radio on, and a few hundred skirts scattered on the carpet. The white velvet couch looked like an abandoned raft. I sat down on it to have tea. "Arianna was asking after you today," Viola said, slipping off one skirt to try on another. It was as if after a week a drum had stopped beating.

"How is she?" I said.

"She's hysterical about you. She says you dumped her just like that and didn't get in touch again."

Well, it had been kind of her to tell it that way. "Everything okay with the sister?"

"Of course. All they ever do is fight and make up."

"She's an unpredictable character."

"She's beautiful, my dear, and beautiful people are always unpredictable. They know that whatever they do, they'll be forgiven." She picked another skirt off the floor. "Oh, yes," she sighed, "it's even better than being rich, because beauty, my dear, never has a whiff of struggle or effort about it, but comes directly from God, and that's enough to make it the only true human aristocracy, don't you think?"

"Very profound."

"It's a simple observation," she said. "All I've been doing lately is observing. Why do you think that is?"

"I have no idea. Have you tried going to a doctor?"

"Arianna would do that," she said, amused. "Ever since she was in that clinic, she hasn't been able to live without doctors. Did you know she was even going to marry one? Then she moved to Rome, and nothing came of it."

"What kind of clinic?" I said. What kind of clinic did I think? One of those horrible places where people go in feeling a little nervous and come out completely crazy. All she did, shut in there, was sleep and play solitaire. When Eva found out, she got on the first train to Venice and brought her to Rome.

I stayed for dinner, of course. "All right," I said, lost in thought. I felt as if it really was me who'd ditched her that morning. "Why do they fight?" I asked after a while. Oh, for a whole bunch of reasons, each one more futile than the last. Plus, you had to remember that when it came to her nerves, Arianna was still a little bit fragile. She couldn't go anywhere without her bottle of perfume and her pack of cards. Once, when she left her cards at home, she'd gone around the streets in tears, did I know that?

"No," I said, "I didn't know that."

"Shall I get dinner ready, signora?" Afternoon had passed and evening was spreading in from the windows. Viola gave a start and switched the light on to reveal a little man with a deep voice, wearing a striped jacket. He had emerged from his afternoon off, looking contrite.

"I think he had a falling-out with the baker's boy," Viola said when he'd gone. "For two weeks now, he's been forcing us to eat crackers, he says they're good for the figure." But I was barely listening to her. "What's the matter?"

"Nothing," I said. The matter was Arianna shut up in that clinic, playing solitaire. The matter was the anguish I felt, that tightness in the middle of my chest. The matter was my undervalued life, which needed changing.

There had been an imperceptible ringing of the doorbell, and five minutes later Renzo appeared. "Good old Leo!" he said, slapping me on the shoulder. "I've been looking forward to a game all day." He was in a good mood, very sure of himself, and very sure that I'd also want to play chess. I stood up reluctantly and sat down opposite him. It was a brief, fierce battle. After two cautious openings, I let my anxiety get the better of me, leading to some tense skirmishes between our pawns and the loss of my bishop. Then I unleashed my knights and managed to draw level, cornering his king in a messy siege. The king seemed on the verge of packing his bags and heading south when the queen, promising some desperate pawns she would satisfy god-knows-what secret lusts, organized a sortie that saved the kingdom. A duel ensued between our rooks, and we exchanged sword thrusts, until, at last, I was run through. Renzo couldn't help snickering. Rubbing his hands together, he called in the servant and ordered a bottle of Chablis.

"Congratulations, darling!" Viola said at dinner, kissing him on the forehead. Renzo shielded himself with exaggerated modesty and she laughed. I watched them. The Chablis was cold and comforting, but not enough to make their smooching bearable. Stuck there in front of the TV all evening, I felt very alone until the presence of the servant, sitting at the far end of the living room, still looking contrite, at last drove me over the edge. I left and went to Signor Sandro's.

Yes, Annamaria had been there, but she'd left ten minutes earlier.

The end of the month was drawing closer and I had to start going regularly to the newspaper office so that I could pay the rent without being forced to camouflage my voice on the telephone. Then one afternoon one of the telephones in the booths rang and Rosario went over and answered it. "It's for you," he said, his face making it clear he had no intention of acting as my secretary.

It was Viola, inviting me to the theater that evening. "Put on your good suit," she said. "We're all going to be very elegant."

"I'm not sure if I feel like it."

"Oh, of course you feel like it," she said.

So I drove home through the evening traffic. I found a note stuck to my door with a pin: *I'm alone, rich, and attractive. How about a Western? Claudia.* I read it twice, then put it in my pocket and phoned the laundry to get my shirts sent over. I did everything with enormous calm. First of all, I switched on the record player, and undressed, then I unearthed a dark suit I'd ordered in a moment of *grandeur* from the Count of Sant'Elia's tailor and laid the pants under the mattress. In the bathroom, I turned on all the faucets because I liked to hear the water running, and lay down in the bathtub to think. When I heard the doorbell ring—my shirts had arrived—I got out of the bath and wrapped myself in a red robe Serena had forgotten to take with her to Mexico. I went to the door, checked they'd sewed the buttons on my shirts, paid, and retrieved my pants from under the mattress. They were perfect. Then I brushed the jacket and the shoes, with different brushes, and dressed with all the care of a bullfighter.

The Diaconos were late arriving, and we walked into the theater just as a girl onstage was invoking her lost youth. It was a totally fucked-up production of *Three Sisters* made fascinating by the desperate attempts of the director and cast to ruin the play and the play's wonderful, ironic resistance. It was such a close-run thing that in the intermission everyone rushed to the bar. The Diaconos' friends were all there, of course, and they managed to be a group even in a crowd of some hundreds of thirsty people. Eva stood beneath a huge crystal chandelier, shaking. By her side, the bird man was holding two glasses, from one of which she took a few distracted sips, every now and again. He had an elastic bandage on his wrist, as if some ornithologist had captured him, then set him free again, but with that sign on him in order to follow his migrations. Arianna wasn't with them. I didn't see her until the end of the show, when I had to throw myself into the mob at the cloakroom to retrieve Viola's coat, and I wouldn't even have noticed her if I hadn't heard her voice. She was crossing the foyer in the company of a fat little man in glasses and begging for a vodka. The only result of her passing was that I lost the good place in line I'd captured for myself near the cloakroom, which meant I was one of the last to reach my target.

"I've seen better cloakroom attendants than you," Viola said as I helped her on with her coat. "Let's get a move on, we're supposed to be going to Eva's for a drink."

"I think I'll go home," I said.

"You just try," she said, and so we went to Eva's place.

It was very similar to the Diaconos', a white apartment building, but the garden was larger, and behind a few hedges an empty swimming pool for the residents lay wide open, waiting for summer. In the living room, there was the usual profusion of armchairs, and a few paintings, including a probably genuine de Chirico and a probably fake Morandi. In the armchairs, the usual people: a serene fifty-year-old whom everyone called by a very long name that was nothing like the very short one by which he was well known as a humorist; a young, left-wing journalist named Paolo, who, it was said, had a secret way with women; and a novelist with a white mustache and a Venetian-style villa in Friuli. Also part of the group were the estranged wife of a TV presenter, who was obliged to attempt suicide every time she wanted to collect alimony; a bearded and spoiled poet, who was heavily involved with the Communist Party; a pleasant foreign correspondent, who'd had a heart attack in Latin America; and an actress, who talked endlessly about Ivy Compton-Burnett. Finally, sitting together on the same couch that evening were a Russian-looking young man with a guitar, a *haute couture* model in love with a homosexual photographer, and an impoverished noblewoman in love with an Alitalia pilot nobody had ever seen. This was the central nucleus, joined for periods of greater or lesser length by other people who were seized on by the group and then expelled in a kind of natural regeneration that guaranteed its continuity. This sort of thing happened mostly in the winter because in the summer everyone went off in different directions. Seaside romances, travel, adventures— any opportunity was good enough for people to go off and do their own thing. But as soon as the sky turned less metallic and hard, as soon as the trees started to sway in a wind that brought clouds, as soon as the days began their headlong rush to the deep purple sunsets of October, the telephones started ringing again across the city, and these people once more sought out one another, exhausted but talkative.

"So, have you expiated your sin?" Eva said. Her familiarity surprised me. "What do you have to say about Arianna?" Arianna wasn't there in the living room and I told her what I'd seen in the lobby of the theater. "Oh, yes," she said, "she was with the director of the show. Arianna always has to involve someone else in her own needs." So she must have told Eva the whole story. Maybe that very morning, after our night together, maybe sitting on the bed, drinking tea and nibbling madeleines. Great! "Do you know Livio Stresa?" she said, grabbing the arm of the bird man, who just then was passing in search of an armrest on which to perch. His name sounded familiar, and it only took me a moment to connect it with a well-known tennis player lately down on his luck. He'd been really good a few years before, even playing in the championship with Pietrangeli, but then he'd stopped competing in the major tournaments. Well, now I knew where he'd ended up.

Arianna came in half an hour later, throwing the door wide open. "To Moscow! To Moscow!" she cried, and judging by the face of the director, who followed her in, it was obvious she'd been parroting that line all the time they'd been together. Her hair was tied back, and she seemed very happy.

"Tell me, Chebutykin," she said, collapsing tragically into an armchair, "did you love my mother?"

"Tell me, Irina," Eva now said, approaching her, "who's that knocking on the floor?"

"It's Dr. Ivan Romanovich. He's drunk. What a topsy-turvy night! Have you heard? The regiment is being transferred!"

"Oh, that's just a rumor!"

"We'll be left alone. My dear, good sister," Arianna said, reaching out her arm to Eva, "I have a lot of respect for the baron, he's an excellent man, I'll marry him, I consent to it, but, I beg you, let's go to Moscow! Nothing's more beautiful than Moscow! To Moscow! To Moscow!"

The director, who was uncomfortable, intervened, saying that she'd mixed up the characters, and the general laughter increased. The writer with the white mustache coughed, as if he'd swallowed part of it, while Arianna and Eva, their eyes sparkling, bathed in their success. They sat down on the same armchair, happy, insolent, and alone.

"Tell me, Arianna," Eva said, glancing over at me, "is that *friend* of yours always so serious?"

"It's just hunger," she said.

"This time it's tiredness," I said.

"Well," she said, "I'm hungry, come with me to the kitchen." She held out her hand and I followed her. Once again we found ourselves in a dark corridor, and then a kitchen, with me again in front of a refrigerator. Life had its still points. Arianna talked, as she stuffed a roll with leftover chicken. "Don't think you can treat me like that, you know," she said. "Why didn't you phone? I had to ask Viola myself to invite you to the theater, how is that possible? No, wait," she said, raising her free hand, "don't answer. Let's go to my room. I hate eating in the kitchen, it makes me feel like a cook."

She led me into a narrow room, the whole length of it taken up with a bookcase filled with books, fashion magazines, records, and a few items of underwear, which she grabbed and put away in a large chest with a shrug. Apart from that, the room was sparsely furnished—a table, cluttered with rulers and set squares and an architecture book covered in a layer of dust, a bed, and on the walls a Klee reproduction and a blown-up photograph of Picasso at his easel. "It was the maid's room," she said, "but since Eva got her divorce, we've done without a maid." A door led to a little bathroom. On the doorpost was pinned a small, handwritten note: *8 a.m. wake and bath, 9 a.m. breakfast, 10 a.m. university till 1 p.m., lunch then sleep till 4 p.m. without cheating, 4:30 p.m. (after cheating) read, write letters home, study especially light subjects, 6 p.m. Eva's store, 8 p.m. freedom, 12 midnight mandatory BED!*

"Don't take that too seriously," Eva said, sticking her head around the door. "Arianna spends her days writing schedules."

"Excuse me, what business is it of yours?" Arianna said.

"It is my business," Eva said, "and it's best if you come back out. As long as you live in this apartment, you have duties as a hostess."

"I have to talk with Leo."

"Leo will understand," was the answer.

They eyeballed each other, while I felt an acute desire to be somewhere else, because if there was one thing I couldn't stand, it was family scenes. Arianna took her eyes away from Eva's face, leaving two red marks on it. "Will you pick me up from the concert tomorrow?" she said.

I asked what concert, and she told me. "If you like," I said.

"What do you mean, *If you like*?" In her voice was the sound of hailstones. A cold wind blew over me, and I took the opportunity to get the hell out of there.

In the living room, I caught an amused look from Viola, but, apart from her, nobody else seemed to have noticed our absence. They'd all gathered around the Russian-looking young man, who was singing Russian-sounding songs. Coming back in, Arianna sat down in the armchair farthest from the circle that had formed around the singer. The anger had left a shadow in her overlarge eyes. I went up to her.

"Is our date still on?" I said, offering her a cigarette.

"*If you like*," she said, taking it.

I noticed that her hand was shaking slightly, but by the time she leaned her head to the lighter's flame, her face had already regained its usual conceited expression.

In the afternoon I went to the movies, to keep warm, but the film was dull as dishwater, and, for the first time, the gaunt faces and secretive shenanigans of the destitute fauna that populate theaters in the afternoon made me really sad. So I left, and started walking down the side streets, with my fists clenched. I had almost an hour left before my appointment, and I was aware, with a kind of fierce clarity, how every minute that passed was one less minute I had to live. At around six forty-five, I went and stood opposite the church where the concert was being given. Music by Mozart. At seven the front door opened and let out a trickle of people that immediately dispersed on the street. I didn't move, just stood there waiting. The door opened again, and two young boys came out, then a few old ladies. Then it stayed closed.

I rushed over to that side of the street. Inside the church, the last musicians were putting their instruments back in their cases, and a priest was moving between the altars, extinguishing the candles. The priest saw me. "It's over," he said. I closed the door and sat down on the steps, not knowing what to do. The city was so empty, you could hear the buildings growing old.

Nothing happened for an hour and a half. Then she arrived. She was in a car, with Livio Stresa. "I'm sorry," she said through the window, "we were on the bed all afternoon, chattering away, and I didn't notice the time," as if knowing this might cheer me up. I got to my feet, brushing the dust off my pants. "Are you upset?" she said as I got in next to her. "Don't say no, it's obvious you're *very* upset."

Livio Stresa was in the backseat. He put his hand on my shoulder. "One thing you should know about both sisters," he said. "As far as they're concerned, whatever time they arranged to meet you is the time they need to start putting on their makeup."

The gesture irritated me. "What if they don't put on makeup?" I said.

He took his hand away and started talking with Arianna again. About Eva, of course, and her store, which is where we were headed.

It was a store only in a manner of speaking, actually a little apartment near the top of the Spanish Steps, not overflowing with trinkets like most places selling antiques, but with just a few pieces of old furniture on display. It was obvious from the start that you only needed to sell one item to have enough to live on for a month, and I remembered my father's shop, with its tiny, patient trade in stamps—the thick catalogs, the magnifying glasses, the tweezers, and that sweet smell of glue that stayed on him even when he was at home.

"Oh my God, is that the time?" Eva said when we walked in.

Sitting in small armchairs were the young, left-wing journalist, the humorist, and the *haute couture* model. She was very tall, a lot taller than the fashions called for that year. They were all drinking aperitifs, and Arianna stole two olives from a saucer.

"We're not staying," she said, handing me one. Eva objected, saying that we were all supposed to be having dinner together. When we left, she didn't even say good-bye. "What a bore," Arianna said as we were leaving. "Why don't you like each other?"

We went to a cellar, near Piazza del Popolo, its walls covered with bottles. Arianna ordered a sherry, but was nervous and couldn't make up her mind to drink it. "How wretched I am," she said. "I never know what to do!"

"Why not play a game of solitaire?" I don't know why I said that, and in that tone. I know all those bottles around us were giving me the urge to drink and I was feeling argumentative. But she didn't react. She didn't say a word. Her courageous face trembled a little, and she put her glass down on the counter. Then she gave me a curious nod and walked out. I didn't move. I took her glass and finished the sherry, slowly, trying to calm down. After a while, I gathered my things and also walked out, stopping at the door to watch the people streaming along the sidewalk.

"Hey." She was behind me, in the shadow of another doorway.

"Listen," I said, "I think I'm in love with you."

"Please don't say that!" she said.

Just then, something happened. There was a soft thud, and a soft sound of rolling, while a woman raised her voice in surprise as the contents of a plastic bag full of oranges rolled across the sidewalk. The woman asked me for help and I mechanically started to look between the feet of the passersby, with much meeting of hands and a lot of laughter.

By the time I'd finished, Arianna had withdrawn even more into the darkness of the doorway. So I turned my back on her, and we stayed like that for a long time, Arianna in the shadows, me sniffing my fingertips, which still smelled of oranges, watching the stream of people, a stream to whose banks we clung.

"Never say that again," she said in a muffled voice. "*Promise?*"

"All right," I said.

"Good," she said, and her voice emerged from the shadows like a brief guitar solo emerging from a band, cautious at first, then increasingly bright, note to note. "Where are you taking me to eat?"

"Charlie's?" I said. It was the trendiest restaurant in town.

"You're crazy," she said, laughing. Then she picked up an orange that had been left on the sidewalk and started peeling it. "Let's go somewhere ordinary and just be close, that'll be enough."

"It won't be enough at all," I said.

I had my rent money in my pocket, and what I wanted to do was spend it all. Which I almost did in a restaurant not far from there. Elegant and expensive, with waiters in dickies, looking stiff. We ordered hearts of palm, pepper steak, and Burgundy.

"It's wonderful to be rich!" she said. "It gives you such a sense of security. In Venice, I didn't think about it, I didn't realize until I came to Rome. But in Venice I had Eva, whereas here I don't have her anymore." Because, obviously, I didn't know how Eva used to be! These days, she'd become a hysterical snob, but Arianna couldn't forget how she'd been when she was younger. God, what a horrible thing it is to get old! She didn't want to get old, *she didn't want to*. It was different for us men, the older we got, the more fascinating we became. I was *too young* for her tastes, did I know that? But women! What a horrible thing it was for women to get old! And yet if it hadn't been for Eva, she'd have died, or gone completely crazy, did I know that? But how could she forgive her for ruining Livio in that way? She'd forced him, with all that flirting of hers, all that obsessive night-crawling of hers, to stay up until four in the morning even when he was in training, until eventually he stopped playing, and when he stopped she divorced him. Because Livio Stresa had been married to Eva, did I know that?

That's what she said, and I remembered how he'd held her glass, in the lobby of the theater, and I realized how fucked-up his life must indeed have been. All the same, I couldn't help despising him a little. Why didn't he get away? What people! All they did was try to leave each other, but they were terrified of succeeding.

"Anyway," she said, smiling to thaw the waiter who was filling her glass, "enough of these sad things. Tell me something amusing, like that time you tried to teach the subjunctive when you were drunk."

"No," I said. "It's best if we get out of here. We could develop some bad habits. How about going for a walk?"

She said that was fine by her, and so we left and started wandering aimlessly, stopping from time to time outside some lighted store window.

"Oh," she said, seeing a colorful, flowery silk dress that seemed to have come into the world just for her, "why aren't you rich? I love buying clothes!"

Even if there'd ever been any possibility of my becoming rich, it had receded quite a lot since I'd paid the check at the restaurant. I put an arm around her waist and she went with me meekly until we turned onto a side street, where I stopped and put my open hands on her chest. There was something poignant about her small, hard breasts beneath her light blouse. She leaned her back against the wall and looked at me with great seriousness. "I beg you," she said, "be kind to me." Then we kissed slowly, repeatedly, each time moving our faces apart to look at each other. It was so silent, we could hear the river flowing under the bridges.

"Let's go to my place," I said.

We were in the shadows once again, and once again her voice

emerged from the shadows, low at first, then bright. "*Are you crazy?*" she said. "I don't feel like making love, haven't you got that yet?" She gave me a last, light kiss on the lips. "Come on," she said, grabbing me by the arm, "a drive will do us both good."

"Are you angry?" she said as we got in the car. "Don't say no, it's obvious you're *very* angry."

She was still smiling, and if she was doing it to annoy me, it worked. Without saying a word, I picked up the Proust book from the backseat. It looked as if it hadn't been touched.

"I want to see something," she said suddenly, turning toward the river. She drove to where all the neo-Renaissance villas were and stopped outside a two-story one surrounded by a vast garden. "Can you smell it?" she said as she got out of the car. "That's the lilacs." I knew the smell well, just as I knew that villa well. It was Sant'Elia's. "Do you like it?" Arianna said. The last time I'd passed it, years earlier, I'd seen a red sign saying it was for rent. The windows had been repainted, and the garden was a lot better tended than it had been back then. It exuded an air of tranquility and privacy that hadn't been there in my day. My general impression was that it was a different place. I didn't like it. "Well," Arianna said, "it may not be Combray, but it's an acceptable substitute, don't you think? Being in a house like this, all you feel like doing is listening to music, tending the lilacs, and making jam."

As far as music was concerned, the place was more appropriate than she could possibly know, but I didn't say anything about Sant'Elia's grand piano, and in any case just then the light came on at the top of the steps and the sound of a Bach chorale reached us. Arianna was on the alert now. Before long, a man appeared in shirtsleeves at the top of the short flight of steps. He was tall and agile-looking, with a semi-halo of gray hair around his sinewy neck. He was like Picasso, only taller, younger, and harder. For a while he looked around, then gave a slight whistle. From the far end of the garden came the sound of loose gravel and barking, then two Great Danes appeared and ran up the steps. "Good boys," the man said, but had to endure their assault. "Good boys," he said again, more sharply, and the dogs crouched, whimpering with impatience, until the man gave them something to eat. "Off with you, now," the man said. The dogs tried feebly to resist, while the Bach chorale grew louder through the open door. "Off with you, now!" the man said again and the dogs moved away, looking at him with infinite sadness, but he turned his back and in a moment it was all over—the man, the dogs, the light, the music. I looked at Arianna. "I come here every evening," she said.

"Why?"

"I don't know," she said. "Maybe because it's a ritual, and rituals always give you a sense of security. There are people who go to church for that. I come here."

"Who is he?"

"Oh, a painter."

"He looks too much like Picasso to be any good," I said, simultaneously remembering the blown-up photograph of Picasso hanging on the wall of her bedroom. What a bummer, it wasn't because of Picasso that she'd hung it on her wall. I was filled with rage. "Come with me to the car," I said.

"I'm sorry," she said, surprised. "Don't you think it's a little early?"

"No," I said, "I'm tired. And besides, if you want to masturbate, you can do it by yourself."

Her face stiffened. "You could at least try not to be vulgar," she said.

"Yes," I said, "I could." Then I didn't say anything more, so she got in the car and we set off. When we reached my old Alfa Romeo I got in without saying good-bye to her. She made as if to say something, then thought better of it, slammed the passenger door, and pulled out, tires screeching. I stood there watching her as she vanished at the end of the street. I was at the end of my tether, truth be told, and, to avoid going to a bar, I went straight home. The first thing I did was switch the radio on, clear the armchair, and move it closer to the table lamp, then I put a cushion where there was a dip in the chair, grabbed the cigarettes that were within arm's reach, opened a book and tried to give myself over to that persuasive inner voice with which we all read. A voice different for each one of us if our souls are different, identical if identical, but in every case perfect, with no false notes, the untrained voice we perhaps have before we come screaming into the world.

*When the doorbell rang, it almost brought the house down. The elec-*tric discharge echoed through the silence of the building with the violence of a seismic shock. I went to open up, my heart thumping. There she was, at the door, smiling at me as if I were Humphrey Bogart. "God, what a racket!" she said, pointing to the bell. "I pressed the only one that didn't have any name next to it." She came in, glancing at herself in the hall mirror. "Oh," she said, shaking out her hair, "I'm *so beautiful*, don't you think?" I didn't reply, and she shrugged, as she walked into the room overlooking the valley. "So, this is where you live," she said, looking around. The apartment was a terrible mess, with the plugs out of the walls, the slats of the blinds dangling toward the floor, newspapers heaped up in the corners, the faulty TV set buried under a pile of dirty shirts. There was even a pair of pants hanging on a door handle. I took it and flung it behind the armchair, but she noticed, which made it even worse. "So this is where you live," she said again, still looking around. "It looks like a shelter. Don't you have anyone to help you? A maid, something like that." She sat down on the bed. "Do you plan to say anything or not?"

"Yes," I said. "If you don't like it, you can go."

She sat there for a moment, stiff and motionless, then looked at her broken-down watch. "I'm sorry," she said, "I realize it's late to be visiting people." I noticed she'd taken off her shoes and had to get up to look for them under the bed. Then I went over and put my arms around her while she still had her back to me. She didn't move. "I came here to go to bed with you," she said, her voice a little hoarse.

We stood like that, rooted to the spot, waiting for something to happen, for one of us to make the first move. In the end I opened my arms and after a moment's hesitation she started to undress. She did so briskly, without looking at me, as if she were alone and getting ready to go to sleep. My heart leaped when she took off her panties. For the first time in my life, I felt bashful.

"What about you?" she said, once she'd pulled the sheet up over her. I sat down next to her. "Are you still angry?" she said gently.

I shook my head. I still had the flash of her body in my eyes and felt intimidated. I turned out the light and started to undress. When I was lying next to her, next to that small, hard body of hers, without touching her, I was overcome with unhappiness.

"Stroke me," she said softly, while the radio brought us moans and groans from the world outside. "Just that, please."

I put my hands on her small, flat belly, but couldn't move her. I was frozen and unhappy and there was nothing in me, not even a little of that warmth I would have liked more than anything else in my life, that all-consuming warmth that would have spread from my belly through my body so that in the end I'd be able to reach her. And that low, imploring voice of hers was even worse. Instead of bringing her closer, it made her even more distant, more unattainable, and I was ice cold, inert, filled with sadness.

For a long time, the radio continued alternating static and

spluttering with distinct bursts of music and it was very late when I got up and switched it off. Arianna had sat up between the sheets. Huddled on the bed, with her back against the wall, she was looking at me in silence. Then I sat down facing her and we sat there staring at each other, scrutinizing each other, until we lay down again. But nothing had changed, and in the end she fell asleep.

Toward dawn, the air turned cooler and the trees in the valley filled with birdsong. Arianna woke up and we lay there listening while the room grew lighter. Then she stood up and got dressed. "Stay where you are," she said, giving me one of those light kisses on the lips. But I went to the window that looked out on the courtyard so that I could keep watching her. She was walking to the gate, stooped against the dawn light. She fiddled with the lock, then got in her car and drove off. I went back to the room overlooking the valley. The sight of the ruffled bedsheets gave me a pang in my stomach, so I tossed everything up in the air and carefully remade the bed. But the sheets still held her perfume. I went to brew myself some tea.

As I waited for the water to boil, I switched on the radio. It was broadcasting old songs and world news. All things considered, it was in good health.

5

I was awakened by the silence. The apartment was full of light, but even though it was almost noon not a sound came through the open windows. Something else must have happened during the night, something that was yet to play itself out. I got out of bed and went out on the balcony. The valley was silent beneath the weight of a still, clear sky and the air was motionless as if waiting for a sign. It took me a while to realize it was the heat.

All at once, I knew what to do. It's strange how a change of season makes us want to be in a different place than where we are. Maybe it's because the air feels different, suggesting other climates, or maybe it's because we realize time is passing and we're standing still. The fact remains that every time the weather changed I felt like getting the hell out. Most of the time I did nothing. That morning I decided to act. I filled a small suitcase with some shirts and a few books and as I sat down for breakfast started thinking about the places I could go with the money I had. There weren't many places and there wasn't much money, which meant there were even fewer places.

I thought about the north. Not Milan—it wasn't a homecoming

that I needed. For some reason, I thought about Lake Stresa, which at that time of year must have been full of azaleas and old people dressed in white drinking orange juice and reading the papers in the shade of the big trees, with Europe peering out from behind the mountains.

"Yes, it's not bad," Graziano Castelvecchio said when he phoned me early in the afternoon. "Whatever you do, don't go to Crete. There's nothing there but stones." He'd come back the previous day, or the day before that, he couldn't remember, but what he could remember was that he'd been looking for me. "Anyway, never make decisions in haste. I'll wait for you here," he said, "it's a real beauty."

The beauty was Piazza Navona, and when I got there I had the usual stupid idea that the sky was more beautiful there than over the rest of the city. I spotted Graziano immediately. He had on one of his legendary white shirts and was sitting in a small armchair at Domiziano's, his pale face turned to the sun, his eyes shielded by a pair of dark glasses. He'd let his beard grow and both his hands were occupied, one holding a glass of beer and the other a glass of scotch.

"Don't drink like that," I said, coming up behind him. "Don't you know alcohol kills slowly?"

"It doesn't matter," he said, "I'm in no hurry." It was an old joke. We kissed each other on the cheeks, and I asked him why the beard. He lifted a finger to get me to lower my voice. "I'm incognito," he said. "Beard and dark glasses. Like a fucked-up cool jazz musician." Not that he did drugs—that was a college students' thing, he said. No, a good *tandem* was better than anything. He was what you'd call a serious drinker. I'd once seen him lift a beer to his lips and pour it down the collar of his shirt. I couldn't ever remember displaying such classic lack of coordination, even in my best moments.

"That's where you reveal yourself," I said. "Nobody drinks in duplicate like you."

"Not true at all," he said, raising the two glasses. "That's another thing that's changed. It's not scotch on the left and beer on the right now, but beer on the left and scotch on the right. I know a thing or two. How are you?"

"Who are you hiding from?"

"From my wife, man. Remember, you never saw me," he said. "But don't think you can bullshit me, I asked how you are."

"How do you want me to be?" I said, letting my gaze wander over the square. "Well, that's what I am."

At that hour, the square was mainly full of old people, kids on bicycles, mothers sitting around the fountain. In the cafés, in the shade of the church, a few customers were drinking coffee and leafing through newspapers. All that was missing were the azaleas and the lake. There wasn't a single face we recognized. Only a couple of years earlier, we would have seen nothing but friends, we'd have talked, turning from one table to the next, with our hands on the backs of our chairs so they wouldn't be taken away from us. Those days were over, only the waiters were the same—the waiters are always the same whatever happens—and when I saw old Enrico, with his failed comedian's face, I ordered an orange juice.

Graziano snickered. "Don't think you can bullshit me, don't think you can pull the wool over your best friend's eyes. I know you shut yourself in the bathroom to have a pick-me-up when the sun goes down."

"No," I said. "That's a lie, and you know it."

"Sure," he said, "I always know when I'm lying. Only, it's sad going home and there's nothing to welcome you back but vitamins. Can you explain why you dried out?"

"Fear of success."

"At what?"

"Dying," I said.

He was silent for a moment, then started lighting a cigar. It took him a while, and when he was done he gave me a dazzling smile. "Good for him," he said. "He knows a thing or two." And he once again stretched his legs on the armchair, which was turned toward the sun. But from behind his dark glasses he was studying two young men at the table opposite. They had well-combed long hair, sandals, belts, and Indian shirts, and were trying to play the flute. All at once, Graziano blew cigar smoke in their direction. "Pennywhistle rebels," he said.

The two young men stopped playing and looked at each other. Then the sturdier of the two held up his flute and said politely, "Want it up your ass?"

Graziano smiled behind his glasses. "Wouldn't make much difference to the sound," he said.

I stood up and put money on the table. I knew what he was like when he got that way, he never knew when to stop. "Can you believe those guys?" he said as we moved away under the covered walk. "But I put them in their place, didn't I?"

"Of course," I said. "You showed them."

"Sure, I showed them, I can't stand these pennywhistle rebels. Did you see how good-looking they are? I bet their teeth would break iron like it was nougat."

His own teeth were small and decalcified. That's what made him look like a poor man still, in spite of his two-hundred-thousand-lire clothes. It's always the teeth that betray that a person was born poor, the teeth and the eyes, and Graziano had known a lot of hunger during the war. They'd had to operate on him twice before they'd discovered that what gave him those pains in his stomach was simply the memory of the hunger he'd experienced as a child.

We'd taken off our jackets and were walking in the sun. "So," I said, "nothing but stones on Crete?"

"And not even a slingshot."

"Big stones?" I said, grasping the fact that once again things hadn't gone well for him.

"Big stones, little stones, stones of all sizes. Fucking boring!" he said as we entered Campo de' Fiori.

We started strolling amid the market stalls. The market was bright and alive with cries—only the statue of Giordano Bruno was grim and silent, but he had his reasons. When we got to Ponte Sisto, Graziano didn't want to cross the river because it would take him closer to his wife, who like all American women in search of local color was in Trastevere.

I barely knew her, Sandie, an abrasive character a dozen years older than him. Daughter of a sausage king, she had brought him, as a dowry, a Bentley, a blue poodle, fifteen-year-old twin daughters, and a faint smell of smoke. Graziano had treated her dismissively, but had had to stop doing that when he found himself incapable of having sex with her. That had happened during a trip to her home in Texas, when he'd realized quite how incredibly rich she was. From that point on, he'd been unable to touch her. The *impotence of shock*, he called it. It was the reason they traveled so much, so that Graziano should find some kind of distraction, but the more he traveled, the greater the shock.

The trip to Crete had been boring as hell. After a month in which he should have finished his novel, he'd met a Greek girl named Niarcos, and they'd gotten the hell out of there together, taking four million lire of his wife's money with them. He'd lost it in a quarter of an hour at the casino on Corfu. The plan had been to double their capital, give Sandie her money back, and vanish to some little island in the Aegean, but Niarcos had disappeared the morning after the debacle at the casino, and he'd had to phone his wife and ask her to come spring him from the hotel, where he was being kept prisoner until he paid his bill. Sandie had arrived with the twins, and when Graziano, as his only justification, had given her encouraging news about his Inert Appendage she'd hit him with her handbag, bruising one eye. "But, Leo," he said, taking off his glasses to show me the eye, which still bore the mark, "she was amazing! Niarcos, I mean. Really hot stuff, like you wouldn't believe. No relation to the tycoon, you know—to the croupier, maybe." He was silent for a moment, thinking about Niarcos. "Anyway," he said, "what can you expect from life when the first thing they do to you as soon as you're born is give you a slap?"

"Very profound," I said. "And?"

"Man, she was one hell of a lay. I assumed that having made progress once, the Inert Appendage had started working again, and thinking it was the only way to calm her down—Sandie, I mean—I grabbed her and threw her down on the bed. A real macho man. If only! There she was, ready to forgive even Jesus, and nothing happened. There I was, thinking about Niarcos like a fucked-up millionaire."

"Well," I said, "these things happen."

"Don't tell me," he said bleakly. Then he understood. "Don't tell me it's happened to old Manolete too?"

"Last night."

"Poor kid," he said, putting an arm around my shoulders. "Is that why you want to get the hell out?" I didn't feel like replying and we sat down on the parapet and looked at the river, which was dirty, placid, and indifferent. "'I don't know a lot about gods,'" Graziano said in a dignified tone, "'but the river is . . .'"

"'I do not know much about gods; but I think that the river / Is a strong brown god . . . ,'" I said. "That's Eliot, man, you can't just quote him like that."

"What are you doing, think you can catch me out? Listen: '. . . sullen, untamed and intractable, / Patient to some degree,'" he said, raising a finger. "But, then, what's that bit about the sea and the river?"

"'The river is within us, the sea is all about us.'"

"Congratulations, man! What are you reading?" When I said *The Iliad*, he raised his eyes to heaven. "Oh, Christ! Listen to this. I'm away suffering the pains of hell, and what's he doing? Reading *The Iliad*."

"I did that so that when you got back, we'd have something to talk about," I said. "Weren't you in the Homeric seas?"

"Big deal," he said. "Just stones."

"What about the sea? How was the sea?"

"The sea?" He thought this over for a moment. "The sea was all about us."

We walked along that side of the river, in the heavy shade of the plane trees. Every now and again, we stopped to look at the view of the two banks, which changed depending on the bends in the river, but each time there were domes and bridges and old buildings drenched in light as if to conserve it for when dusk came, until Castel Sant'Angelo came into view, darker and more compact than the rest, with the corroded angel at the top.

"We have to do something," Graziano said. "What are you planning to do?"

"I told you."

"There's no point, man. You have to make a decision. You can't just go on like this."

"What are you doing?" I said. "Are you starting now?"

"Sure," he said, "I'm doing it for the salvation of your soul. You can't go on like this," he said again, pointing to the angel. "What will you say to the thirtieth-birthday angel when he appears before you with his flaming sword and asks you for the last time what you intend to do with your life?"

I told him I would set my guardian angel on him. "It's his business," I said, "and he's really angry."

But Graziano was lost in thought again and said nothing.

We walked on as far as Piazza del Popolo. There, in every bar, we found a message from his wife, which Graziano ignored, securing the complicity of every bartender with an astronomical tip. Whenever he did so, he'd take a mouthwatering wad of money from his jacket pocket.

"The novel is dead," he said suddenly on our way out of one of the bars.

"They all say that."

"I mean mine," he said. I was sorry to hear that—it had been the one thing keeping him going. "Too difficult, too pointless. We have to start doing something substantial, otherwise what'll we tell the angel?" He raised that thin finger of his. "You should know by now how things really are. Do you want it to be your best friend who tells you how things really are?"

"As long as he's gentle."

"I've developed a theory. They're great inventions, theories, much better than practice. Look around you," he said as we walked down Via del Corso, surrounded by people coming out of office buildings. "Is there anything you feel part of? No, there isn't. And you know why there isn't? Because we belong to an extinct species. We happen to still be alive, that's all," he said, stopping to light a cigar. Because, if I didn't know, we were born just when beautiful old Europe was fine-tuning its most lucid, thorough, and definitive suicide attempt. Who were our parents? People who slaughtered one another on the battlefields of countries that no longer existed, that's who they were. We were born between one furlough and the next, and the hands that had stroked our mothers' loins were dripping with blood—not bad, as images go—or else we were the children of the old, the sick, the senile. The wrecked or the wreckers. We had the most fucked-up parents in history.

"Speak for yourself," I said, but then I recalled my father's silence, as he repaired the chair in the kitchen on the very day he returned home from the war, and I fell silent.

You just had to look around, Graziano went on. Having returned home, our heroic progenitors threw the most opulent, festive, vulgar funeral banquet in the history of mankind. They made more children, those same pennywhistle rebels who were now replacing us. And what about us? We were an ugly memory, survivors of the slaughter, and we just had to be content with the leftovers.

"When we like them," I said, thinking of the bowl of peanuts at the Diaconos' apartment. Then I thought of my old Alfa Romeo and the apartment overlooking the valley. It was true, everything I possessed was someone else's leftovers. Except for Arianna, and I didn't possess her. "All right," I said, "couldn't we survivors put these leftovers together into a juicy hamburger? I'm hungry."

"We can," he said, "but when your angel appears, what will you do, will you offer him ground beef and onions?"

"And a lettuce leaf," I said. "What else would you suggest?"

"A movie," he said. "Let's make a movie, what do you say? The story of someone who, when the angel asks him what he wants to do with his life, goes home and kills his father." He thought this over for a moment. "Or else let's make a nice Western," he said. "Which would go down better right now?"

"A Western," I said. "I already have a title, *The Last of the Mohicans*, what do you think?"

"God, I can never talk seriously to this old faggot," he said. "Can't you be a little bit serious for once?"

"Who's putting up the money?"

"Now you're just being negative," he said, sitting down on the Spanish Steps. "Sandie, who do you think? As soon as I can provide her the necessary guarantees. Couldn't lend me a dildo, could you?"

There were azaleas on the steps, great vases of azaleas everywhere, in addition to the painters, the hippies, the tourists, the necklace vendors. A limpid Roman evening was settling over the roofs, and the wind wafted the scent of the flowers to us and ruffled our shirts. Graziano fell silent, wilting, as he watched the traffic circling the fountain. The wind stirred his beard, and his cigar, which he was gripping weakly between his teeth, turned red at the tip.

The city was caressing us. Gradually, it became less difficult to think about Arianna. Basically, nothing irreparable had happened. Nothing irreparable ever happened in this city—sad things, maybe, but not irreparable ones. And anyway, if I was going to leave town, I wanted to see her. At this hour, she must be in Eva's store, playing solitaire.

"Let's get the hell out of here," I said. "I know some people nearby who could offer us a drink."

"Leftovers," he said, "nothing but leftovers."

Graziano pulled himself to his feet and followed me up the steps until we got to Trinità dei Monti, then we took the street that went downhill, leading to Eva's store. We climbed the front steps, holding on to the railing, then pushed the glass door. A bell rang as it opened. The humorist was there reading something aloud, along with the fashion model, Livio Stresa, and Paolo, that journalist with the special way with women, sitting next to Arianna. I was greeted as if it were the most natural thing in the world for me to be joining them.

It wasn't an unpleasant situation. I made the introductions, while Graziano, suddenly concerned with etiquette, struggled with his jacket, searching for a sleeve. "How are you all?" he said. Arianna smiled. This confused Graziano for a moment and as he tried to walk over to her, buttoning up his jacket as he did, he slipped on the rug and almost fell. She laughed. Up until then, I hadn't realized how drunk he was.

"Why don't the two of you sit down?" Eva said. "That seems safer."

But I said we had to leave right away, we had an appointment.

Graziano looked at me in surprise, then joined in the game. "Sure," he said, puffing at his cigar butt, "a whole bunch of appointments. That's what we're like."

"Just for a while," Arianna said, abandoning her cards. "*Please!*"

"They said they have things to do," Eva said. The others said nothing, looking at us with conciliatory smiles.

"But they *only just arrived*!" Arianna said.

Something in her voice hit Graziano in some particularly sensitive spot, because he again looked at her and the smile faded on his lips. "Whose are you?" he said, without taking his eyes off her. Someone laughed, which annoyed him. "What's the matter?" he said. "Can't I ask a question?" Then he suddenly fell silent, swayed, and looked around for support. The only thing at hand was a little table with a Chinese vase on it, which wobbled alarmingly. For a moment, we all grimaced, as if hearing the smash. Seeing Eva look so ashen cheered me up and I took Graziano by the arm and walked him over to a chair. "Never sit down," he said, raising a finger. "Nobody may come to help you up." Then he moved me aside to get a better view of Arianna. "What shall we talk about?"

"The subjunctive?" she said.

"Where we're going to dinner, you, me, and Leo," Graziano said. "This is Leo. My best friend."

"I thought as much," Arianna said.

"But didn't you have an appointment?" Eva said, her lips still pursed even though she'd recovered from her fright.

"Canceled," Graziano said. "All our appointments have been canceled. Why don't you come along too? Let's all go eat some leftovers at Charlie's. Charlie's leftovers are the best in town."

"Drop it," I said. "Maybe another time."

"That's what you always say. You can't fool me, you always know a thing or two."

"I guarantee it," Arianna said.

"All right, all right," he said, raising his finger. "Never insist. It isn't good taste. I'm getting up now," he said, starting to summon his legs.

I tried to help him, but he pushed me away, and so we all sat there watching his resurgence. He managed to stand on his third attempt, and Arianna gave a little laugh. "If you want something done, do it yourself, right?" she said.

He looked at her. "I always do it myself," he said.

He kissed her hand, then Eva's, then the model's. All very proper, truth be told, but by now too late to save face. All we could do now was get the hell out of there, as quickly as possible.

Arianna walked us to the door. "How are you?" she said to me in a sweet tone.

"How do you want me to be?" I said. "I'm fine."

She stood there watching us as we walked down the stairs, which didn't make things easier because Graziano kept turning his head to look at her. Outside, things went better. The evening wind revived him. "Whose is she?" he said again.

"Nobody's."

"That's impossible. Isn't she your girl?"

"No."

"Amazing," he said. "Right now, I'm going to go home, take a shower, and come back for her." Instead, we went to a trattoria on Via del Babuino and he walked in and asked in a loud voice for the best leftovers in the house. Then he plunged headfirst into a huge plate of macaroni in cream sauce. He ate quickly, in silence, as if giving himself a transfusion. "Don't expect me to buy that," he said all at once, raising his head from the plate. "She's your girl."

At midnight we ended up in a disco, a dark, noisy place like all places of that kind, full of ghosts. We'd chosen a table a long way from the speakers, but it wasn't any use and we had to scream in each other's ears to make ourselves heard. I'd have liked to leave, but Graziano had his eye on a big, phosphorescent cube in the middle of the room where some long-legged girls were dancing. There was one of them he particularly liked. All at once, he threw himself into the mix, insisting that I follow him. For a while the three of us danced, but the girl didn't seem to mind. Actually, all the people there were doing their own thing, as if they were in a skating rink. All at once, another girl materialized from the darkness, having been wandering through the room on her own, and now there were four of us.

We managed to keep them with us even when the music granted us a break and we walked back to the table, and Graziano ordered a bottle of champagne, which the girls started drinking as if it were orange juice. They weren't bad. Very sure of themselves, truth be told.

"Allow us to introduce ourselves," Graziano said. "Gazzara and Castelvecchio. The last of the Mohicans." One of the girls asked if that was a band. "Oh yes," Graziano said. "We're banned everywhere. More champagne?"

But they preferred to dance, and we followed them back onto the floor, determined to enjoy ourselves. Soon afterward, taking advantage of the fact that we were an even number and that, after all, we'd all shared champagne, we tried to embrace them, but they didn't like our hands on them and they wriggled out of our grasps and continued swaying gently, which made things worse. By dint of insistence, we managed to keep them still for a while when the DJ had the bright revivalist idea of putting on an Elvis Presley song from a dozen years earlier.

"Hear that, Leo?" Graziano said, winking at me over his girl's shoulder. "Good old Elvis!"

But the girl freed herself with an impatient gesture. "Do they still play seventy-eights here?" she said to her companion. They preferred to talk between themselves.

"Records are the only things progress has slowed down," I said as we walked back to our table. It struck me as a good topic of conversation, but when I put it to the girls it fell as flat as some observation about the weather. As they drank, they kept glancing around the room.

"Christ, girls!" Graziano said. "Let's talk about something. You make me feel like some fucked-up seventy-year-old, with all this champagne, and the two of you constantly holding your noses in the air."

They looked at him in surprise and might even have said something if a long-haired young guy dressed in red velvet hadn't suddenly appeared at our table and held his hand out to Graziano's girl. "Are you coming?" he said. The girl was getting to her feet when Graziano turned pale and, before I could do anything, threw himself on the young guy.

In the darkness and confusion, nobody noticed that there was a fight at our table, not that it lasted very long anyway. When Graziano sat down again, he'd lost his dark glasses and his shirt was torn.

"Who is that asshole?" the young guy said loudly as he was dragged away by the girls.

We were left on our own. "I'll show him," Graziano said breathlessly. "I'll show those pennywhistle rebels. What is this—I provide the champagne and he nabs the girls? I'm going to take a shower, then I'll go find him and smash his face in."

But he was all in. He was slumped in his chair, panting, too weak even to hold his glass. It took him quite some time to recover. For a while he sat staring into the darkness and biting his lip, then he stood up and headed for the bathroom. But he stopped in the middle of the room and climbed into the big phosphorescent cube. When he was up there, he didn't move. He stood there for a while looking down at the floor a couple meters below. By the time I figured out what he was planning to do, it was already too late. It wasn't the first time I'd seen him pull that stunt, but I thought at least by now that was something he'd had enough of. He swayed a little on the edge of the cube, then dropped to the floor face-first.

I elbowed my way through the crowd. He was lying facedown on the linoleum, so still it was quite scary. Someone touched him on the shoulder with that cautious revulsion with which we touch strangers who get sick in the middle of the street. I turned him over as gently as I could. His beard was smeared with blood. "Lucky Strike," he said calmly. That was all he smoked at such moments. I passed on the request to the waiters nearby and before long a Lucky Strike arrived. I lit it and put it between his lips.

"Let him smoke it," I said to the waiters, who wanted to get him back on his feet. "He'll get up when he's finished."

And, in fact, it wasn't long before he asked me to help him up. I walked him to the bathroom, waited at the door of the stall while he finished throwing up, then washed his face with a handful of wet toilet paper. He had a black-and-blue bump right in the middle of his forehead. "Christ, what a knock," he said, touching himself with his fingertips. "Feel it, it's throbbing like a heart." I also tried to clean his shirt, but that only made things worse. "Forget it," he said. "I have a whole lot of shirts." To get out, we had to go back across the room, but he didn't want me to help him. He was walking very upright, his trunk stiff. After a suicide attempt, you always need a lot of dignity.

He refused a taxi and we set off on foot, but he immediately grew tired and we had to sit down on the steps of a basilica that rose imposingly in a deserted square. He lit a cigar and let his gaze wander along the outside wall of the basilica until he saw a little door. He got up and went to see where it led. We found ourselves in a cloister enclosed by columns carved from boulders.

"Christ," he said, "more rocks."

Above us were high brick vaults, open to the sky in places, and looking up you could see the starry heavens, divided into circles, ellipses, and triangles, like one of those maps showing the trajectories of the planets. We were looking around when in the silence we heard someone knocking on glass and a monk appeared at a lighted window. "What do you want?" he said in a soft, kindly voice.

"Which floor is God?" I said. Graziano, in the shadows, laughed quietly. The monk was silent for a moment, not sure how to respond, then jerked his thumb upward. "In the attic," he said, "but he's asleep right now. Do you want me to tell him anything?"

"Yes," Graziano said, "tell him we looked for him but couldn't find him. Now it's up to him to find us."

"Try to come here during the day," the monk said. "Now go, but remember to close the door. Good night."

"Did you hear the brother? He knew a thing or two," Graziano said when we were back outside. "Where do you think we can find a taxi? I'm at the end of my tether." When we found one, we collapsed onto the seats. Graziano started humming the Presley song. "Man, what a giant!" he said every now and again. "There's never been anyone else like him, right, Leo? You know what we're going to do now? We're going to Sandie's, we'll wake her up and tell her she has to finance our movie."

"She'll shoot us down."

"No she won't," he said. "She's a woman of the world, didn't you know that? She knows I'm the man of the house. In a way, at least. And besides, there are no guns in the place."

There was no need to wake her. Sandie was up, and didn't even let us in past the entryway, which was almost entirely occupied by a Ping-Pong table. Graziano looking as wrecked as he did merely increased her anger. Where had we been? What had we been doing? Sandie's face was covered with some kind of cream, and there was a kerchief wrapped around her head. She wasn't at her best, in terms of appearance, but she didn't care.

I found it hard to defend myself from her attack. Graziano, smiling slyly, had gone and sat down in the one armchair in the room and was looking at us in silence. "Shall we talk seriously?" he said.

"Now's not the time, Graziano," I said.

"Talk seriously about what?" Sandie said. "This *is* serious! Who pays the bills? Who pays the bills all day long? I don't support your friends, and I want to know who pays the bills."

Sitting on the Ping-Pong table, the two twins, who were also still up, watched us in silence, chewing gum. Graziano noticed them and started saying, "What are you two still doing up?" but saying it in every possible tone—soft, paternal, worried, irritated, imperious. He was like an actor trying out a difficult line. Then all at once he took his belt off. For a moment I thought he was going to use it on the two bovine figures on the table. Instead, he buckled it around his head and slumped facedown on the armchair. It was his treatment for hair loss.

"Look at him!" Sandie said furiously. "What does he need his hair for?"

"I have no idea," I said. "To comb it?"

Graziano chuckled, and even I couldn't refrain from a little smile. Given the hour, it wasn't a bad joke. Sandie, though, didn't appreciate it and started yelling. "Faggots!" she said. "Faggots!"

At this point I decided I would get the hell out of there. I bowed, then stopped at the door and asked Graziano if he wanted to come with me. He still had his head down. "No, Leo," he said, "I only just got back, and Sandie would be offended." So I left him there looking at life from the most bearable position.

But I was at the end of my tether, truth be told, and when I found myself on the street, heading for Ponte Sisto, I started to kick the garbage cans, overturning them on the cobblestones. The river was black and in the distance the beacon on the Gianicolo pierced the sky at regular intervals. On Campo de' Fiori they were already setting up the market stalls for the next day and I took two apples from a pile of crates and ate them as I walked toward Piazza Navona. The fountain glistened motionlessly on its blue base in the middle of the deserted square. The square was magnificent at that hour, as if aware of its own splendor and its own pointless survival. I settled down under the arches and sat there looking at it, waiting to feel the desire to go home. But the desire didn't come and so it occurred to me to go to the sea. The deserted streets urged me to start up my old Alfa Romeo. I got there in less than half an hour.

It was vast, immense, dark. I went and sat down at the end of a jetty. The sea was all about me, the waves beating on the shore, and, in the distance, in the darkness, the lamps of the fishing boats winked. What did old Cavafy say? The city will follow you, he said. For elsewhere, he said, do not hope, there is no ship for you, there is no road, just as you've wasted your life here, in this little corner, you've ruined it in the entire world. He knew a thing or two, that old Cavafy. I smoked a couple of cigarettes and thought about the packed suitcase I'd left at home. Well, I'd arrived where I meant to arrive. Now all I could do was turn back.

From some very distant place, the sky was starting to lighten by the time I got home. Outside the gate, a little English car was parked. I knew it well by now. And the girl who was inside it, fast asleep in her seat. "Arianna," I said, "what are you doing here?"

It took her a while to figure out where she was. Then she tried to smile. "Oh, Leo!" she said. "I was afraid you wouldn't come back."

6

Summer arrived unexpectedly early. At the beginning of May, a cloudless Egyptian sky dominated the city for some days, until we found ourselves, almost by magic, in high summer. The cafés threw their glass doors wide open, beneath the awnings along the river the jukeboxes started to scream out the songs nursed during the winter, and hundreds of buses deposited hordes of tourists in front of the ruins. The long, wearying Roman summer had begun and I had made up my mind. I'd asked Renzo Diacono to get me work in TV. He'd cheered up and invited me to lunch at Charlie's, where he got me to fill out an application form and told me all the good things I'd be able to do once I was hired. He was certain I was the right man for the job. He didn't specify what the job was, but he was absolutely certain.

In the meantime, I went to the sea every morning with Arianna. She couldn't stand beach resorts, all *those people* under their umbrellas with their portable radios, so we'd preferred to scour the coast northward in search of quiet spots and a little clean water. We'd found it, but most of the time, in order to get to it, we had to climb over the perimeter wall of some still-uninhabited villa, and there, on the sun-drenched concrete terrace, surrounded by the rocks of some private dock, we'd put our towels down and start to read while waiting to take a dip.

"It's true," Arianna would say, "there's always such a sense of security when you have a villa. Do you think you'll be able to buy me one sooner or later? I really need a villa." Then she would sigh, stretching out in the sun.

At first she brought her architecture books with her, but she usually preferred to play a little solitaire, lying there motionless, cultivating her own laziness. Ever since I'd started reading *Swann's Way* aloud, the architecture books had vanished from her beach bag, to be replaced by a pillow she put under her head to be more comfortable while she listened to me.

It was nice to read in the sun. Around noon, wearing only my pants, I'd drive to the nearest village and buy sandwiches and beer. By the time I got back, she'd be peering into the villa through the windows or she'd already be in the water if the excessive heat had helped her overcome her fear of swimming by herself. She was terrified of seeing her shadow follow her on the seabed and usually swam on her back. We'd leave around three in the afternoon. At some of the villas we felt so good, we'd leave a note of gratitude on the door.

Back in town, I'd go to the newspaper and stay there until dinnertime, then go wait for Arianna at the top of the Spanish Steps, surrounded by taxi drivers playing baccarat on the hoods of their cars, flower vendors, and tourists. She was usually late and I'd kill time by reading the book I had in my pocket, but at the end of each page I'd look up to see if she was coming. And there she'd be, walking lazily through the crowd, her nose wrinkled in disgust at the exhaust from the cars and her arms crossed to support a never-opened architecture book. She'd look around, searching for me, then, seeing me, she'd slow down even more and, holding back a smug smile, stop at a store window, or walk twice around a lamppost, or turn to look insistently at some tourist dressed in a ridiculous manner. At last she'd reach me and give me a distracted kiss. "Well," she'd say, "don't go thinking I love you."

Sometimes we'd go back together to Eva's store, which meant having to spend the evening with all the others. It didn't happen often because by now it was obvious that my relations with Eva were as cold as could be. The time I'd gone there with Graziano had seen to that because if there was one thing Eva couldn't stand it was drunks and, to top it all off, she'd found out that I too had once exercised the same vocation. Whenever we were all together, I'd avoid speaking to her and would spend my time chatting with the Diaconos, or the writer with the white mustache, or sometimes even the fashion model, but only to see Arianna squirm until I stopped. After that, she wouldn't talk to me for an hour.

Most times, though, we managed to be alone and we'd have dinner in some open-air trattoria or other and then wander through the city, which was cool and animated, teeming with adventures and rendezvous outside the bars and around the fountains. Usually, we'd roam in search of baroque churches, because Arianna was thinking about a doctoral thesis demonstrating how superior Borromini was to Bernini, and one way or another we always ended up outside the Oratory of San Filippo, pallid under the streetlights, as bloodless yet elegant as a lady who consumes nothing but tea. Although I didn't understand what the baroque had to do with the hydraulic problems of saving Venice, I would follow her in these wanderings of hers, kissing her in the cavelike entrances of churches, her lips as cool as her breasts, then ending up at my apartment, where we slept together until dawn, when she would leave so that she could be found in her own bed when Eva woke up and get ready for that day's excursion to the sea. Until, one morning, we found as many as four villas occupied by their rightful owners and we realized that that was the end of that.

One of the first evenings in June, Renzo informed me that in two days' time I could start work. The following morning I made an inventory of my clothes and realized I didn't have anything suitable for the occasion, so I decided to invest the money I still had left in a new suit. In a surrender—nobody's sure why—the loser is always more elegant than the victor, to obtain better conditions, maybe, or maybe when you have nothing left you realize that appearances are at least something, so I went on a tour of the downtown clothing stores. I found a white suit like Graziano's. True, it wasn't the same linen—in fact, it might not have even been linen—but it produced the right effect. I put it on, then and there, and went to Signor Sandro's to phone Arianna. "There's news, I have to talk to you," I said, explaining where she could reach me.

"Talk now," she said. "You surely don't think I can hold out until I see you."

"Try to survive," I said, "it's worth it."

She arrived no more than twenty minutes late, walking along the sun-drenched sidewalk. Her heels penetrated my heart. She was wearing a dress with white and blue stripes and was the freshest thing I'd ever seen.

"Wow! Get a load of you!" she said loudly, looking at me. "So, what's going on?"

"What are you drinking?" was all I said.

She wanted a *granata*, she was *crazy* about *granatas*, so I ordered two of these specialties of Signor Sandro's, crushed ice with rum and exotic fruit juices served, depending on the quantity of sugar, in a coconut or a bamboo bottle. "One Perverse Virgin *granata* and one Bamboo," I said to Signor Sandro and Arianna giggled.

"A very suggestive combination," she said. She had never thought about that combination before, and I too giggled like an idiot as Signor Sandro began the ritual preparation. Arianna, who was always fascinated by ritual, watched him with close attention.

When he noticed, his moves grew even lighter and more elegant. Then he placed the results of his magic in front of us and stood waiting for the verdict. Arianna bent over her straw and sucked two or three times, then raised her big, half-closed eyes and smiled. Signor Sandro returned her smile and bowed his head. They had understood each other.

"Now, that's a bartender!" she said loudly as, freezing cold and a little drunk, we walked back out onto the street. "I'm *crazy* about him!"

"Of course," I said. "Aren't you crazy about all old men?"

"No beating about the bush, what do you want to tell me?"

But still I kept her on tenterhooks as we walked in the direction of Piazza San Silvestro. She was so nervous, she insisted on crossing when the lights were red. We walked into the remainder bookstore and started moving down the aisles, separately, but from time to time I raised my head and looked at her, against the colorful background of the books, with her impatient profile and her hair that kept getting in her face, and that's the most *significant* memory I have of this whole story, if not the most beautiful, until we emerged as if from a maze, unsteady on our feet, and found ourselves at the exit, where I gifted her a copy of *Under the Volcano*, which she never did read.

"Come on, now!" she said, at the end of her tether. "Are you ever going to tell me what all this celebrating is about?"

"I'm getting my head together," I said. "As of tomorrow, I'm working in television."

She stood quite still, staring at the photograph on the book cover, the one of Lowry on the shore of the lake with his frayed white shirt and sad goatee. "I don't know if I like that," she said at last.

"Why not?" I said.

"I don't know," she said. "You're you."

And, with this incontrovertible statement, she put an end to the subject and refused to talk about it for the rest of the after-noon. To do something, we went window-shopping on Via Frat-tina, but she looked at the displays without seeing them. She was very nervous, and when we went to dinner at the usual open-air trattoria she ate listlessly.

"Why are you doing it?" she said suddenly.

"Because I'm tired of leftovers."

"What does that mean?"

"I know what it means," I said.

She fell silent, playing with the base of her glass. It was damp and she was using it like a rubber stamp, leaving rings on the white paper tablecloth. "Are you sure you're not doing it for me? I don't want you to do it for me."

"I'm doing it for myself," I said, "only for myself."

"Oh, all right, then," she said.

We sat for a while in silence, though I felt like screaming, and when I asked for the check I did so in too loud a voice. Arianna stopped playing with her glass and took hold of my hand, gripping it tightly.

"Shall we go to your place?" she said.

She was scared, she hated any kind of change, and we'd had such a great May. I was struck by the sudden hope that at last everything would go right, that tonight would finally be different. But it didn't work out that way. Once again, we found ourselves in my bed, wearing ourselves out with caresses, listening to each other's bodies, begging each other, looking for the word that was never uttered—*Don't go thinking I* love *you*—until dawn found us clinging to each other, as inert as a couple of lobsters.

"Wow, look at that suit!" Renzo said, getting out of his Mercedes in front of the TV center.

As an opener, it couldn't have been more unfortunate. In the morning sun my suit was reflected in the glass of the building as if it might shatter it, while all around us was a whole crowd of executives in blue jackets with pipes in their mouths. Christ, I stuck out like a sore thumb.

Inside, things went a little better because in the artificial lighting my suit didn't stand out quite so much. To make up for this, it was almost cold and the nervous sweat the suit had made me break out in chilled my back as I followed Renzo along a corridor lined with doors. We stopped at one marked *Personnel Office* and went in without knocking.

"Hello, Signor Diacono," a female employee said, coming up to us. "Hello, Signor Gazzara." Clearly, they were expecting me. The employee was an efficient young woman who as soon as we came in had slipped an index card into her typewriter. "Surname?" she said, even though she'd just used it. "First name?" She went on to ask my father's name, and I thought about him, and my mother's, and I thought about her. Then she asked where I was born and I thought about my gloomy city, then the date of the happy event and I thought about my birthday three months earlier drinking hot caffè lattes in a bus terminus at dawn. "That's all," the young woman said with a smile that brooked no reply. It was humiliating to be classified.

Renzo slapped me on the back. "Let's go to your office," he said, going ahead of me into an elevator that would take us to the room where within a month I would be earning a figure I'd never seen, at least not all at once, in my life.

The office was long and narrow and occupied by two tables, at one of which sat a pleasant woman in her forties who got to her feet when we walked in. I shook the hand she held out to me without catching her name, although I assumed I'd get to know it in time. Besides, I wouldn't have to spend much time in that office and sooner or later I'd end up working with Renzo.

For a while my friend lingered, singing my praises. The woman listened admiringly, throwing me the occasional knowing glance, which I returned with a modest smile. We would probably end up bowing to each other, I thought, and something like that did happen when Renzo, after another little slap on the back, left to go to his office three floors up.

"Are you a graduate?" the woman said as soon as we were alone.

"Yes," I said. "I have a degree in patience."

"Then you'll do well here," she said, laughing. "Besides, there are so many morons here, as long as you're not an idiot people think you're a genius." This must have been a code phrase, so I didn't say anything while she explained our work to me. It consisted of drafting press releases about the shows currently in production.

While she said this, I thought about the world outside. Was anything wrong? "It's cold in here," I blurted out, massaging my arm.

"Oh yes," she said, "the air-conditioning's quite powerful, it always has that effect the first time. But we can't do anything about it, it's a general system."

"Long live the General," I said, but she must have exhausted her reserves of humor for the morning because my subtle one-liner didn't raise even the hint of a smile. Instead, she handed me a package of press releases so that I could learn the style.

I'd read better things, but I continued leafing through them until the fatigue from my sleepless night with Arianna and the rarefied climate finally gained the upper hand and I began to genuinely shiver with cold. I started to wonder if by any chance I could get an empty Ballantine's bottle from the staff bar. But where to find hot water? Was *anything* hot in here? As for using it, I could have done so surreptitiously, below the table, holding it in my lap. Like an old man in a world where all his friends are dead.

"You know what you could do?" my colleague said as I looked out beyond the wall of glass at the sun beating down on the streets. "You could go to Signor Laurenzi's office and get some information from him about the latest TV series being imported from America."

"That sounds like a good idea," I said with the appropriate enthusiasm. "Where would I find him?"

"Room 212. If it's not a good time, just wait."

"It's always a good time for me."

"I meant for Signor Laurenzi," she said.

I stood up, my face turning red. If he didn't have time, I'd hurry to the bar, no two ways about it. I left the room and immediately got lost in a maze of corridors and rooms all clustered together, where I could see secretaries at work and executives with their feet up on desks, smoking pipes and watching TV sets. There was also a whole bunch of people strolling arm in arm through the corridors, leaving a trail of mild tobacco smoke behind them. I kept pushing doors that were windows, opening windows that were storage closets, and pressing buttons for elevators that were out of order. After a while I gave up, stopped by a real window, and looked out at the inner courtyard. In front of me was a reddish, transparent façade, subdivided with the regularity of a chessboard, and each square was an office, some with a lamp on the desk, to indicate that it was the office of someone in charge of something, and the higher you climbed, the more lamps there were, because, as we know, the higher you are, the easier it is to be in charge. In desperation, I stopped a girl and asked her where Signor Laurenzi's office was. She was one of those girls who go around as if they're the only people who can see anything, and she looked at me as if I were an idiot, then pointed to an usher, who reluctantly put down his *Corriere dello Sport*—ah, the good old days—and led me to my destination.

Signor Laurenzi was there, in person, when I walked into his office. "What's up?" he said. He might have been around my age, but there wasn't a hint of generational solidarity in his eyes. While I told him what was up, he focused on my white suit as if it were a shroud. "I don't have time," he said. He looked like someone who'd already met his angel and given him the answer he deserved. I told him I'd wait for him. "Not here," he said and I asked him if the bar would be all right. The sociability of my answer surprised him. He looked at his watch. "All right, in the bar," he said, "in forty-five minutes."

Now I just had to find the bar, but I let myself be guided by instinct, took the first elevator that was leaving, and pressed the top button. When the door opened, I was immediately hit by a comforting clink of glasses and bottles. I followed the call and ended up in a vast room whose glass walls granted a view of the surrounding city. I ordered a tandem and sat down on one of the stools lined up along the window.

After an hour and a quarter, Laurenzi still hadn't shown up, and the more time passed, the more obvious it became that he wouldn't show up. But he'd told me to wait, so I waited.

In the meantime, I observed the crowd at the bar. Most of them were executives with pipes. It set an impressive tone, having a pipe, and they chattered away, banging their pipes in the ashtrays or else sucking on them with their thumbs over the chamber or else rummaging inside them with a match, morbidly so. It was a scene of intense activity, tobacco pouches, fingers grabbing, pressing, twisting. They gave off a good smell as I looked at their blue jackets, their shiny shoes, their moderately weird ties, and their pipes.

I turned to the window and looked out at the city. The sun was beating down on Monte Mario, where my apartment was, with its balcony looking out over the valley. It must have been hot out there, at the insurmountable distance of a few inches of greenish glass.

I decided that a second pick-me-up was more than justified and I was on my way to the bar when I saw the director I'd met with Renzo at Signor Sandro's. He was wearing the same military greatcoat and possibly the same hangover. Without even wondering if he would recognize me, I went up to him. He looked at me through half-closed eyes, making an effort. Then he said, "Do you still answer for your own life?" He'd remembered my line, with the pitiless memory that alcoholics have for trifles.

"No," I said, "not today."

"Right," he said, looking around. "It gets harder every day. What are you drinking?" Then he saw the two glasses. "Christ," he said, "you know all about it." He was drinking straight Pernod. At eleven in the morning. Holding our glasses, we made our way through the people to the window, with him constantly having to greet this person or that and be patted on the back by people who called him by his first name, Corrado. "What are you doing in this place?" he said, climbing onto a stool. He touched the glass as if testing its solidity. I said I was working there too. "I punched it once," he said, lost in thought, "and broke two knuckles. And what work do you do?" I told him. "Two knuckles, I kid you not. Why don't you come with me to the studios? You'll come back filled with news and glory and get a prize for fieldwork, simple as that."

"Okay," I said, excited by the idea of getting out of this place. We slid off our stools and walked to the elevators. He leaned on my shoulder with one hand, keeping the other free to shake hands with people. In the elevator, since he didn't know anybody in it, he leaned back against the wall. When we came to an abrupt halt on the ground floor, the slight jolt made him open his eyes again.

The big atrium was deserted and the ushers were chatting among themselves as they checked people's passes. I was afraid they'd take my pass away and ask me where I was going, but nothing like that happened and we pushed open the glass doors and found ourselves outside in the heat of the sun.

The studios were a couple of kilometers away and we took my old Alfa Romeo. Corrado looked at the traffic with his eyes reduced to two slits and his elbow out the window. The wind blew in, whirling alcohol fumes around the car. You could get drunk just by sitting next to him. "It's not as bad as it seems on the first day," he said suddenly. "You'll get by, you'll see." It was surprising that he'd guessed what I was thinking. I said if the worst came to the worst I'd buy myself a pipe. "Right," he said. "Apparently that works, except that when it falls in your glass it's hard to fish out."

But there were few guys as fucked-up as he was. At the studio gates the ushers greeted him like one of them. Inside, it was no different. Everyone he met greeted him as if they were the best of friends and offered him a drink, but as soon as he turned his back they smiled because even if he was the greatest director television had ever had, the only one who could go into the CEO's office without knocking, they all knew that his time was up and there was nothing special about greeting him.

By about one o'clock, he was completely gone. The corridors were full of bizarrely dressed people because they were in the middle of shooting two historical series. We saw a bit player dressed as one of Napoleon's soldiers leaning against a bathroom door.

"Good man," Corrado said to him, opening the door, "did you do it for your Emperor?"

The man looked at him without understanding, but gave a stupid smile anyway. "Hello, chief," he said.

"You know the story of Napoleon's soldier?" Corrado said sleepily as he used the stall next to mine, making a mysterious amount of noise as he did.

"Yes," I said.

It was the story of a lancer at Austerlitz who advanced ahead of everyone else, amid the smoke and the cannon fire, until he lost his legs and arms, but still continued to advance fearlessly, crawling across the field with the flag between his teeth. That evening, in the hospital, Napoleon gave him a medal, and asked him if he had done it for his Emperor.

"No," said the soldier.

"For your flag?"

"No."

"For your country?"

"No."

"So why did you do it?"

"For a bet," the soldier replied.

"A nice story," Corrado said, "very instructive."

Then he fell silent, and after a moment I heard a dull thud and a groan. I rushed out of my stall and into his. He was leaning against the wall, holding a swollen, bleeding hand to his chest. He had punched the tiled wall and was looking at me with eyes full of tears and astonishment. I was going to help him when I realized he was about to throw up. Just in time, I managed to get him to bend over the bowl.

"Oh, Christ!" he was moaning. "Oh, Christ!"

Then I realized he wasn't the one moaning, I was. When he turned, he almost fell on top of me. It was an embrace, but mainly it was the need to cling to something that wasn't the toilet bowl.

"Sit down," I said, "I'll go call someone."

But he was shaking his big head. "Who are you going to call? There's no one to call." He was weeping. "We don't have anyone anymore! We don't have anyone anymore!"

All at once, a huge, frightening sob echoed around the tiled walls of the bathroom. I looked at him, startled. Christ, how could someone allow himself to get in such a state? Instinctively, I started to retreat until I found myself in the doorway. "I'm getting the hell out of here," I said. In the corridor I spotted Napoleon's soldier. He looked worried. "Call someone," I said, and hurried to the exit. On the sidewalk, I stopped for a moment to warm myself in the sun. Then I got in the old Alfa Romeo and drove to Piazza Navona.

The square was flooded with sunlight. It was break time, and I sat down at Domiziano's and ordered some cheese sandwiches, hoping to see Graziano. Every now and again, I'd look up at the church clock. The sandwiches were edible, but the thought of going back to that building took away my appetite. I smoked one cigarette after another and watched the hands of the clock move. By half past two, things had turned serious; at a quarter to three, after a final attempt to stand up, I closed my eyes and counted to a hundred. When I opened them again it was too late to get back in time and I knew that instead of that glass building I would go to the offices of the *Corriere dello Sport*. The thought of the pleasant forty-year-old wondering where I'd ended up amused me. Then I ordered another beer and started eating the sandwiches, thinking about how to save face.

"Christ, what a getup!" Rosario said when I walked into the newspaper office. "You look like someone."

"Yes," I said, "Lord Jim." Then I asked him if the offer of a permanent job was still open. He thought it was, but we'd have to wait until the head of department arrived. He was pleased. He liked the idea that we'd be working together, because with all these girls around he felt like a rooster in a henhouse, and also because we'd be able to split the night shift. Even the head of department, when he arrived, was pleased that I'd made up my mind. He was a blue-eyed pit bull who kept his hands on the armrests of his chair as if constantly having to restrain himself from jumping on you. He put me straight to work, and I hammered away like a fury at the type-writer, transcribing one article after another, until the end of the shift, when the girls suggested opening a bottle of bubbly. "We've trapped you," they said, but they were pleased too.

The worst part came when I found myself on the street with an empty evening in front of me. I couldn't go home because Renzo would be looking for me and I still had to think of a valid excuse, so I made the rounds of the bars on Piazza del Popolo, looking for Graziano, but he seemed to have melted away. Then I thought of Claudia. I hadn't heard from her since she'd left that note on my door. I'd have liked to see her, but I hesitated. Not that I thought I'd annoy her by showing up—too much time had passed since we'd had our affair—it was more that her life had gone in a direction where there was no room for me anymore. That kind of thing happened. In the end I bought a bunch of flowers and went to wait for her outside her building.

It was on a little square in the back streets of Trastevere and she arrived at dinnertime, carrying a plastic bag filled with provisions. She was wearing pants and a blue sweater. Her clogs, which she always wore in summer, made her swing her hips even more than usual, and her erect back emphasized the roundness of her breasts. I let her walk past me without seeing me, then followed her up the steps and grabbed hold of her bag. "Gazzara!" she said loudly. "Flow-ers!" She threw her arms around my neck and we stood there like that, hugging while the doorman looked on. She pulled away and looked me in the face, closely. Whatever she saw, she said nothing. She took the bag and the flowers and continued up the stairs. From the haste with which she did this, I realized she was really pleased to see me.

In the apartment—I walked in by myself while she went to pick up Biondella from the neighbor—I was struck by the usual smell of smoke, cooking, and eau de cologne I knew so well. I went to the window. The promise of a long, mild summer evening hung over the little square, where the waiters stood between the tables of the trattorias, waiting for the first customers to arrive.

"What a suit! Where did you steal it?" Claudia said, coming in. One more remark about my suit and I would take a pair of shears to it. Claudia handed the little girl over to me and I took her and went and sat down on the couch. She had grown in those months, with that slow, inexorable premeditation unique to children. She was unsure whether she recognized me, but in the end she sat there and we started playing while Claudia made dinner. After a while, with her usual wisdom, she came and took the kid from me and put her in her playpen. She treated her with tender ease, and as she bent down, seeing those two blond heads close together made me think what rotten luck the guy had had who'd gotten her pregnant before marrying her and then gone and died in a motorcycle accident.

"How are things at school?"

"Tough," she said. "Like walking through a minefield."

"Still fighting with the other teachers?"

"Oh yes," she said as I started looking at the bookshelves to see if there was anything new. I found Dylan Thomas's letters to Vernon Watkins. "To hear him, you'd think Thomas owes him everything," Claudia said. "It's true, though—it's always a bad idea to die before everyone else. Take that work of mine off the table, dinner's ready," she said. I removed her pupils' exercise books from the table. We'd spent some good evenings, once upon a time, doing the marking together.

"What wine do you have?" I said.

"The best discount bulk wine I could find."

"Forget it," I said, slipping out the door. I went back out on the street and managed to get a bottle of already chilled Soave at a trattoria.

"This was Hemingway's favorite wine when he was in Venice, did you know that?" Claudia said as we sat down to dinner. For some reason, this made me feel emotional. "What's the matter?" she said. "What a face you're making." Then she put a hand on my arm. "No," she said, "don't tell me."

The little girl was asleep and we ate in silence, listening to the noises coming in through the window. When the phone rang, Claudia gave a start and raised her head. She let it ring several times, looking at me. Then she went to answer it.

"Hi," was the first thing she said after she lifted the receiver. She had her back to me, and for a while all I heard was yes and no. "Yes," she said abruptly, "but not this evening, I'm sorry." The person at the other end insisted and she gave a little laugh. "I'm sorry," she said again, "but I really can't. Tomorrow, yes. I'm sorry."

It was difficult for me to hold on and not signal to her that I was going. It was also dishonest, but I was in no position to allow myself to be honest. When she came back and sat down, her face was red. "The thing is," she said, "he loves me . . ." I searched desperately for something witty to say but couldn't think of anything, so I kept quiet. "Are you staying?" she said, putting her hand on my arm again.

"If I may."

She nodded, lost in thought for a moment, then crossed her elbows and, in a single movement, pulled her tight-fitting T-shirt up over her soft, full, naked breasts. My heart started beating again in my chest. It had seemed motionless for months. Still silent, Claudia stood up from the table and took off her pants and her red panties simultaneously, with that dancing pace that I loved in her more than any other thing, and as she passed Biondella she gave the girl a brief caress. She pressed a lever and the couch folded out into an already made-up bed.

I felt her arms around my neck and her fingers in my hair, I put my forehead between her breasts, and we stayed like that, motionless, until her fingers began, lightly, curiously, to explore my body, recognizing me. Then, with an angry little cry, she started moving her hips. It was a slow movement of enticement, as ancient as the undertow on a beach, and I felt a forgotten languor spreading from my numbed belly. "Oh, Leo!" she said softly. "My dear, dear, dear Leo!" She stopped for a moment, just long enough for me to grab hold of her, then started swaying again, caressing me and saying over and over, "Come, Leo, come, come, come, my dear . . ." until, as if at a sudden blow, she quivered, arched, and planted her nails in my back.

I collapsed into sleep but awoke a few times during the night. One of those times, Claudia was smoking in silence, stroking my hair, while sounds came through the open window, voices in the trattorias on the square, the clatter of dishes, the melancholy sound of an out-of-tune trumpet. I lay there, motionless, and listened until I fell asleep again.

I slept until late morning, when I woke up to an empty apartment. I found coffee already made, along with a note. *Stay as long as you like.* I thought about it, as I lay in a bathtub filled with warm water, I thought about whether to stay or not, until I realized that the only thing I could do now was leave and never come back. And so, like so many other times, for the last time I got out of her bath, dried myself, finished the coffee, and left, firmly closing the door behind me.

7

Sitting on the terrace of his apartment, against the background of a red sunset crisscrossed by hundreds of swallows, Renzo was very understanding. He said he should have known from the start that it wasn't the right job for me. It was embarrassing: one minute more and he'd be apologizing to me.

"Anyway," he said, "it was a nice dream. Let's forget about it."

Viola's little laugh came out a tad forced. "I fear you're really incorrigible, Leo!" she said, before once again devoting her attention to the bare foot with which she was pushing the swing seat she was lying on, drinking grapefruit juice.

In the silence that followed, I had the feeling this whole business had cost Renzo more than he was letting on.

"Is the gentleman staying for dinner?" the servant asked, appearing among us with his usual murderous silence. He made no secret of his sympathy for me and at table always insisted on serving me twice.

"No," I said, "I have an appointment."

It wasn't true, but when you smell gunpowder in the air, a dignified retreat is the best solution. Neither Renzo nor Viola insisted, so I stood up and took my jacket. Renzo simply asked me when I might be available for a game and Viola walked me to the door. "Phone Arianna," she said before I left.

"Has something happened?"

"No, nothing," she said, "but you know how she dramatizes."

So I went to Signor Sandro's bar to summon up the courage to call her. I spent the whole day trying, but always stopped before dialing the last digit. Despite a stiff pick-me-up, I just couldn't do it, not even from Sandro's, so I had a burger and went to the movies. Then I went back home and started reading again and it was two in the morning when, despite the hum of the radio, I heard her steps on the stairs. I went to the door and opened it before she could ring the bell and bring the house down. She must have poured a whole bottle of perfume over herself. I saw immediately that she was hysterical.

"I'm hysterical," she said as she came in, then looked at me. "I thought the TV people must have given you the night shift. I was waiting for you outside here until five."

Why didn't she drop it, she knew perfectly well what had happened. "Drop it," I said, "you know perfectly well what happened."

"Me?" she said. "I don't know anything." Passing the mirror in the entryway, she reacted with annoyance, because although she couldn't under any circumstances get by without looking at herself in the mirror, right now she was so hysterical she couldn't even bear her own image. She kept going as far as the armchair and sat down on the book I'd left open. "Well," she said, looking around her but as usual without drawing any comfort from it, "how does it feel to have gotten your head together?"

People going around remembering things I'd said was something I was starting to find hard to take. Arianna continued looking at me, while I felt almost physically the presence of the book under her thighs. As if she'd read my thoughts, she shifted just enough to pull it out and throw it on the floor. I felt anger overwhelm me.

"Pick up the book," I said.

"No," she said, "I'm not picking it up."

"Pick up the book," I said again.

She looked at me defiantly. Then she bent down and picked up the book, but as soon as she had it in her hands, she couldn't resist, she tore it in half and threw it back on the floor. When she looked at me again something in her was broken. "I'm sorry," she said, her eyes full of tears. "I'll buy you another copy, all right? I'll buy you another copy!" I turned my back on her and stared at the wall, trying to control myself. "I was so worried," she said. "I thought something had happened to you." Her nails were digging into the palms of her hands.

"Nothing happened," I said. "I just couldn't take it, that's all." I gathered the scattered pages of the book from the floor.

"Couldn't you have made an effort?" she said.

"For who?" I said. "For what? You yourself said that I'm me."

"It's not true!" she said, tears in her eyes. "You're not a screwup."

"Who said I was?"

"Nobody," she said hastily. "Nobody said it."

"I found work as a journalist," I said. It took guts to define my job at the *Corriere dello Sport* like that, but I felt I had to boost myself in some way.

She looked at me uncertainly. "Really?" she said. "You mean that sports paper hired you?" I said yes and she passed a hand across her forehead. "Oh, all right, then," she said, calming down. She sat down again in the armchair. "Can I stay here?" she said. "I don't know where else to go."

So she'd quarreled with Eva. "Have you quarreled with Eva?" I said. It was like taking the lid off a pressure cooker.

She really couldn't stand it anymore! She was tired of Eva behaving like a queen bee! Did I know that now she'd started flirting with that man, that humorist with the big nose, just because a comedy of his had achieved a modicum of success? How could anyone be such a stupid snob? Livio was literally devastated, and did I know what she did? She embraced that other man *right in front of him*! And then she went around passing judgment on everyone else, *her of all people*! What was I doing now?

"Listen," I said, pausing in the middle of undressing, "I'm going to bed." I was at the end of my tether, truth be told. "You do what you like," I said. "If you don't know where to go, there's the armchair, but stop all this nonsense, it makes me want to throw up. And don't come here and tell me you were worried about me."

"I really was worried about you."

"All right," I said, "all right. What do you want us to do? Do you want some brioches or do you want to go to the sea? Well, I'm going to bed. I'm tired of being your lightning rod." When I said this, her eyes again filled with tears, but she didn't say anything, and I went to bed, turning my face to the wall so as not to see her. I guess she couldn't stand the sight of me either, because she switched off the light. The room was suddenly flooded with moonlight.

What a night! A cool breeze came in through the open window, along with the distant sound of crickets, but she didn't move from the armchair and I didn't call to her. We stayed like that for a good part of the night until I fell into a light half sleep filled with dreams. Toward morning, waking with a start, I looked over to the armchair. It was empty, and the room smelled vaguely of lilacs.

And yet it was nice to leave home in the morning with everyone else. It made you feel a straight-up kind of person. In my old Alfa Romeo I drove into the city, down a steep slope lined with trees so dense they gave you the feeling you were going through a forest, then left the car in a parking lot and continued on foot. The city, beneath a fresh, bright sun, was animated in a different way than the pinched, febrile animation of the night, and the traffic didn't have the tragic cheerlessness of the afternoon. Gangs of small children released from school were playing in the shade of the monuments, and in the doorways of stores housewives were talking in loud voices, waiting for the heat of the afternoon. The cafés were being kind, in their own way, thanks perhaps to all that milk overflowing from the cups of cappuccino, and only the cold brioches made me sad for a moment. I'd given up on the pleasure of breakfast at home and had it instead in the café near the newspaper offices, where Rosario was waiting for me so that we could play pinball before going into work. Even the absolute stupidity of the work could be tolerated, especially as it didn't usually start until an hour after we arrived and we had enough time to read the papers, smoke a few cigarettes, and chat with the girls.

That same afternoon, while I was transcribing the account of a friendly soccer match that had ended, much to our correspondent's dismay, in a fight, I again smelled the scent of lilacs. With my eyes fixed on the keyboard, and my ears blocked by the headphones, the only thing I had at my disposal to connect me with reality was my nose. But there was no mistaking it: *Coeur Joyeux*. I spun around. Arianna was behind me. She'd been in the neighborhood and had thought to drop by to see me, wasn't I pleased? "We were so stupid last night," she said. What was I writing? I stood up to introduce her to Rosario, and keep her at a distance. We were alone in the big copy department. "Keep working," she said, sitting down in the head of department's armchair. "Don't you have air-conditioning here?"

Rosario was excited. Of course—Arianna was wearing that blue-and-white-striped dress and smiling enough to dazzle him. I too was on tenterhooks, but for a different reason. I was afraid she would eventually discover that all I was in this place was a fucked-up typist. I started typing the article again, as quickly as I could.

Looking up from time to time, I could see her and Rosario chatting, while she looked with curiosity at the booths, with their cork walls and obscene scribbles, the thin brown discs for recording copy, the magnets for cleaning them, the typewriters with their pedals and headsets. When one of the telephones started ringing, Rosario went to answer, and Arianna was again behind me. I sensed her presence growing heavier as she stood there reading the nonsense emerging from my typewriter. "It isn't exactly Proust," she said.

"It isn't me either," I said, performing an act of self-destruction.

"You mean to say," she said, when I'd explained to her that I was only transcribing someone else's article, "you *never* write anything that's yours? They *never* send you to cover something and write about it? You never do features, in-depth articles, that kind of thing?" She may not have known anything about newspapers, but there was no way I could make her believe I was the editor. I saw a possibility for salvation in the fact that Rosario was coming back. But it was like clinging to a lead life jacket, because once he'd caught what we were talking about he offered to explain to her in detail the way the department worked. I started typing again, while still keeping an eye on Arianna. She was bravely trying to keep a smile on her lips, but every time she turned to look at me it fell to earth before reaching me. I finished my task satisfactorily and joined them. "A job for students," Arianna was saying, to which Rosario replied that students did in fact give us a hand on Sundays, when there was more work.

"Order something at the cafeteria," I said to Rosario. But Arianna said she had to go, she had errands to run. She'd put on her dark glasses and was searching for her purse. She passed by it a few times before she saw it. One of the telephones rang and I went to answer it. By the time I got back she'd gone.

"Strange girl," Rosario said. "What do you think happened to her?"

"Nothing. Why?"

"She looked as if she was about to start crying, didn't you see?"

"You're wrong," I said. "Don't think about it." But I couldn't think about anything else and when I left I started walking the streets, knowing I'd lost her. I wanted to get drunk, I wanted the most god almighty hangover I could manage, because I could stand anything except losing Arianna after disappointing her like that. I had to find Graziano. I would find him even if it meant going around all the bars in the city and I began with the ones on Piazza del Popolo, only finding people who'd see him. From what they told me, I got the impression he was having one hell of a party. One person told me he'd seen him with two bottles in his jacket pockets to sustain himself on his journey from one bar to the next, another that he'd tied a kerchief around his thigh, and a third that he'd seen him heading for Piazza Navona but doubted he could make it all the way there.

Knowing Graziano, I didn't take any notice of this and drove to Piazza Navona in my old Alfa Romeo. I left it in a parking lot because I didn't know when I'd be able to pick it up again and continued on foot. The evening was cool, the temperature suitable for drinking without ice, and my stomach in good condition. It was likely to be a memorable encounter.

But I was still on the embankment when I realized it wouldn't be easy to find Graziano. Buses were parked everywhere, which meant the square would be overrun with tourists. I hoped they wouldn't disgust him so much as to send him elsewhere, to Santa Maria in Trastevere maybe, but that was unlikely, it would be too close to his wife. The square was indeed full of people, and what with the tourists, the painters of views, and the parties, you couldn't walk without bumping into someone. At Domiziano's, Enrico told me he'd seen him an hour before, looking for a free table, then asking for a glass and leaving. He couldn't have gone far, and I started moving between the toy stands and the painters' easels while monstrous balls shaped like caterpillars rose, whistling and twisting, into a sky illumined by streetlights.

I found him sitting on the rim of the central fountain, on the side facing the church, where there were fewer people sitting. The kerchief was now knotted around his forehead and he was sitting with his feet in the blue water. He was pouring scotch and beer into his glass, adulterating the mixture with a little water from the fountain, and drinking it. It was clear that he needed help.

"Leo, my boy," he said, watching two tourists photograph the fountain, "how sad to feel one is part of a herd." He raised his glass in their direction.

"From the last of the Mohicans?" I said.

"Yes, from the last and most fucked-up of the Mohicans. When are we making our movie?"

"Tomorrow," I said. "Let's start tomorrow. This time for real, but right now let me take you home."

"Home? I'm not going home," he said, raising a finger. I told him he could come to my place if he wanted and he looked at me genuinely touched. "What would I do without you?" I tried to help him up, but he wouldn't let me. "Impossible," he said. "Why don't you sit down instead? I have some things to tell you. The time has come for you to know, my boy . . . Have you ever watched butterflies in the spring? Well, with children, it's different . . . No, that wasn't what I wanted to tell you. For some time now, I've been thinking I have some things to tell you. What were they? . . . Oh, yes, I had a declaration to make to you. Leo, you're a great guy. Don't say 'no,' let me speak. You're a great guy because you have to be a great guy to quit drinking. How's it done?"

"Try to pray," I said.

"I don't pray," he said. "At most I say 'please.'"

"All right, now let's get out of here."

"I told you no. I told you I have a declaration to make to you first. Then we'll go to your place. Or wherever you like. You're a great guy, but I already told you that. You're a cat. You keep to yourself and you could care less about this dirty, low-down, fucked-up world. You don't need a rich wife. No kidding, I admire you a lot. If I were a fag, I'd fall in love with you. Wouldn't we make a lovely couple?" he said as I put his shoes on him. "It's the Appendage that bothers me, the Inert Appendage, the Irreversible Pendulum. Am I turning gay? Sometimes I think I am and I'm scared of turning gay. Why don't you turn gay too? You can do it for a friend. What do you have to lose? We'll turn gay and then at least we'll be something. This way, what are we now? We're nothing, not even fags."

"We'll take our time and think it over," I said, "tomorrow," meanwhile cursing myself for having left the car so far away. I knew I wouldn't manage to get him all the way to the parking lot, so I got him to sit down on the sidewalk at the far end of the square, repeating to myself that he wouldn't move. Then I ran to fetch the old Alfa Romeo.

It took me a while to get back because the tourist buses had all started to leave and were blocking the intersections. When I reached Graziano, I found him fast asleep right where I'd left him. I woke him up enough so I didn't have to take him in my arms to put him in his seat and then I drove home. It was a problem getting him up the first flight of stairs to the elevator. "What would I do without you?" he kept saying, genuinely touched. "You're better than my mother, that's for sure." I managed to put him on the double bed, the one I never used. "Christ," he said, "I'm at the end of my tether," and fell asleep before I even had time to take off his jacket. He still had his bottle of Chivas Regal in his pocket and I brought it with me into the room overlooking the valley. I took a glass, filled it, and switched on the radio. Then I threw myself into the armchair and started drinking, alone.

The morning after, my head felt as big as the room I was in and it wasn't easy to get it through the door of the kitchen to make coffee. I brewed it in industrial quantities, then woke Graziano.

"Did we at least have fun?" he said, taking his cup of coffee in both hands. He was shaking. He asked for the sugar bowl and ate a few spoonfuls. "I dreamed all night about our movie," he said. "When shall we start?"

"Not today," I said, "tomorrow. Today my head's full of sand."

"Have you been drinking? Tell me the truth, you've been drinking. The old boy has been drinking, now that's something to celebrate. Got any left?" he said, rubbing his hands.

I'd had some left, but I'd poured it down the sink when I made coffee because just the sight of the bottle made me want to throw up. "Let's talk about the movie," I said.

The problem was Sandie, but he said he would work on her in the appropriate way. He just had to hold out to her the possibility that the Irreversible Pendulum would begin working again. As a start, we established that we'd go to the movies every night to study the question from the technical point of view, camera angles, reverse shots, and all that crap, he said. We would start that very evening. For now, he had to go home and calm Sandie down. Where was the phone? He dialed his home number but didn't say anything, just to gauge from Sandie's hello how much venom she was spitting, then, apparently reassured, he took a bath, combed his beard, lit a cigar, and left.

I didn't budge from the apartment until it was time to go to the office. All day long I jumped every time the phone rang. On one occasion nobody spoke at the other end, but I couldn't be sure it was Arianna. Toward evening it got to the point where I couldn't stand it anymore—it's always harder to stand things when evening comes—and I phoned her at home, but there was nobody there. Then I tried Eva's store. Arianna wasn't there either.

And, no, Eva didn't know where she could be. She was sorry, she said.

I saw Arianna two evenings later, coming out of a movie theater. I was with Graziano and she was with Livio Stresa, who looked even taller and thinner than usual, in blue jeans and tennis shirt. For a moment I thought about joining them, but I didn't move. Maybe it was Arianna's pale face that held me back or her head held too high, I don't know, maybe it was the fact that they were alone and holding hands, all I know is that instinctively I stopped and stood watching them walk away through the crowd. Arianna turned in my direction before getting in the car, and her big, anxious eyes searched the crowd for a moment.

"But I know her," Graziano said, by my side. "What an amazing leftover. What do you say? Shall we take a shower and go looking for her?"

I phoned her the next day.

"It's you," she said.

"I have to talk to you," I said.

"I have to talk to you too," she said.

I went and waited for her at the top of the Spanish Steps, as usual. But this time she didn't arrive late and didn't stop to make a tour of the streetlights on the way. This time she came straight toward me. She was wearing dark glasses. She stopped by my side and looked down the steps toward Piazza di Spagna. They were full of people sitting, waiting for the evening wind to start blowing, and the big bunches of azaleas were wilting in the heat. Arianna was silent for a while, holding on tight to the book she had in her arms, but her hand was opening and closing nervously. "Before you say anything, I want you to know I've slept with someone else," she said.

A few days later, when the paper put me on the night shift, we started working on the movie. Graziano showed up at my apartment at nine in the morning, clean-shaven. "New life, new look," he said. "Have you hidden all the bottles?" He'd promised he wouldn't drink until six in the evening for all the time it took us to write the screenplay. "Oh, Lord," he said when I put a bottle of orange squash in front of him. "I'll never manage to drink so much water. You wouldn't have any leftovers that are more fun, would you?"

"Don't forget your angel," I said.

"Oh, well," he said, sitting down at the typewriter, "I get the message."

And so began our battle with the thirtieth-birthday angel. It would last a long time, almost until the end of July. For a month and a half, we worked every day until sundown, naked to protect ourselves from the blasts of heat coming in through the window, breaking only for lunch, to eat some sandwiches and then sleep for an hour in the sunbaked apartment. Every once in a while, we'd take a shower, then get back to the typewriter.

The story of the thirty-year-old who killed his father was coming along well, and sometimes Graziano would get to his feet, clap his hands, then rub them together. "Good, good!" he would say. "Now, how about we have a little pick-me-up so that when we get back to work we'll be sharper and brighter?" But he mainly said this to hear me say no, even though I knew perfectly well that as soon as I left the room he'd take the opportunity to have a slug. Then, around sundown, we'd go out on the balcony and look at the valley while Graziano drank his tandem. "How can you resist?" he'd say. I was at the end of my tether, truth be told, because in the evening I still had to go to the newspaper and, all in all, I never slept more than four hours a night. Sometimes I was so exhausted I'd fall asleep at the typewriter at work until I was awakened by the phone ringing.

There was one advantage, though, which was that I didn't think about Arianna. I didn't want to think about her, but every time the phone rang at home I'd clench my teeth until I knew who was on the other end. Since that evening at the top of the Spanish Steps, when I'd left without saying a word, I hadn't heard from her. Then, after a couple of weeks, the front doorbell rang. Graziano and I put our pants on, wondering who it could be. It was her.

"Well," she said, smiling in that conceited way of hers, "what are you doing, aren't you going to ask me to come in?" I stood aside. She hesitated a moment, then shrugged and came in, glancing at herself in the mirror. "But there are *two* of you!" she said ecstatically, catching Graziano with a bottle in his hand.

"Shall we have a drink?" he said nonchalantly.

I took the bottle from him. Arianna recognized him even without his beard. "Why don't we have dinner together?" She was very beautiful, of course.

"Right away," Graziano said, looking at her spellbound. "What movie have you stepped out of?"

She smiled and collapsed on the bed. "What a day!" she said. "I got up very late, went to the swimming pool for three hours, then went back to bed for another two hours. I'm exhausted."

Graziano was looking at her, forgetting to breathe. "A very productive day," he said.

"Why?" she said. "I produced red blood cells, *isn't that enough*?"

Graziano fell silent for a moment. Then he said, "When shall we get married?"

She laughed. "Not before September. I have to take a vacation first. What are you two doing?"

"We're writing a movie."

"What kind of movie?"

"A traditional avant-garde movie," Graziano said. "It's about a guy who, when he turns thirty, goes home and murders his father."

"How about if he murders his sister instead?" Arianna said. She was flirting, she'd always liked flirting, and every now and again I caught her glancing at me. Without saying anything, I went and sat down at the typewriter. I couldn't say a word, not even when, around seven, before leaving, she asked if she could come see us again. But from that day on she came every afternoon. Around six she would ring the bell and come in, with that insolent air of hers, always looking slightly different, maybe with a new blouse, or pair of pants, or sandals, or else just her hair combed in some weird way. She'd wander around the room, looking at herself in the mirror wherever there was one, and regularly end up on the bed, playing solitaire. Sometimes she'd make tea, and we'd have it on the balcony, still warm from the sun. She'd flirt shamelessly with Graziano, light his cigars, make sure there was ice in his tandem, force him to tell her *something amusing*, and listen with her eyes wide open. And then, around seven, she'd go, liberating the mirrors.

"Christ," Graziano would say, "why don't you ever talk to her?" But from the window I could see her car and the bag with the tennis racket on the backseat and I knew that when she left us it was to join Livio Stresa.

Our last day's work left us with a big void that we tried to fill with a dinner. I asked the paper if someone else could take my shift and set off for Signor Sandro's, as arranged. Arianna and Graziano were waiting for me.

"How do you feel?" she said.

"Tired but unhappy," I said.

I was pleased when she replied, "Even Graziano here isn't so cheerful. You both look quite fucked-up," she said, adopting our jargon. "I don't understand, didn't it come out well?"

"Please," Graziano said, "don't use verbs like *come*. How about a pick-me-up?" he said next, holding out his glass to me.

"I want one," Arianna said. "I want to get drunk tonight."

"Why?" he said.

"Because Leo doesn't love me anymore," she said.

We took her car. The sweltering heat had emptied the city, but in Trastevere the trattorias were full of people and guitar players. We chose a place that was fashionable at the time, where you sat on church pews to eat. We had a long wait before we were served and we killed time with a couple of bottles.

Our morale started to improve. Even Arianna drank a lot, and the more she drank, the more her eyes glittered. They must have given off more light than the candles on the tables because there wasn't a man in the place who wasn't looking at her. "And what if she says no?" she said.

"I'd like to see her try," Graziano said. "I'll take her on a cruise and if she says no I'll refuse to perform my conjugal duties. What do you think, Leo?" Because he hadn't yet found the right time to talk to Sandie about the movie.

"Sure," I said. "No woman can resist if you catch her at the right time, and there are plenty of right times on a cruise."

"It's the only place there are any," Arianna said.

"Sure," Graziano said. "I'll ask her one moonlit night on the Baltic. 'Darling,' I'll say, 'do you want to help me out financially?' How about you, what are you going to do?"

"Oh," Arianna said, "I'm still not sure. I'm supposed to be going with my brother-in-law to some friends of his who have a villa by the sea." That's what she said.

"Everyone's going away, only Leo is staying here," Graziano sang softly. "The old alley cat! He knows a thing or two."

When we finished dinner, we decided to do the rounds of the bars and Arianna insisted Graziano and I sit in the backseat of her car. The wine made her drive fast. "Two famous filmmakers and their delightful Girl Friday die tragically on the Muro Torto," Graziano said, breaking off from singing Elvis Presley to himself. "I just had an idea. How about we go to that disco and look for our two friends? What do you say, Leo?" I said nothing, abruptly grabbing hold of my seat because Arianna had turned the wrong way onto a one-way street at high speed. Miraculously, we dodged a few cars and had almost gotten to the end of the street when we were stopped by a red signaling disk. Immediately, two carabinieri approached us with their hands raised to their caps—but that was the limit to their politeness. "License," one of the two said to Arianna.

"*Please*," she said, and started searching under the dashboard. She searched for a long time, much longer than was necessary, while the two carabinieri waited in silence. At last she made up her mind to find the license and held it out through the window. One of the two took it.

"Are you sure you gave it to the one who can read?" Graziano said serenely.

We ended up at the station house. What happened was, they also knew that joke about how stupid carabinieri are supposed to be and when they asked Graziano to repeat what he'd said he told them the whole joke. Instead of laughing, they made him get in their car. We followed them.

At the traffic lights Graziano waved to us and on one occasion leaned out the window. "They don't have the slightest sense of humor. What do you think, Leo? Shall I tell them the one about the old lady and the electrician?"

When we reached the station, I started to follow them inside, but they wouldn't let me. "Don't worry, Leo," Graziano said as one of the two carabinieri took him by the arm. "If they hit me I'll scream. Anyway, I'll give you custody of the twins."

We sat, waiting. Arianna was very nervous. "What'll they do to him?" she said. "Couldn't he have kept his mouth shut?" I didn't reply, just sat there looking at the streetlights. I could smell her perfume and feel her eyes on me, like a weight. I had to make an effort not to turn to look at her. She kept staring at me, then said, "Do you love me, Leo?" She said it warily, in a low voice.

"No," I said, still looking at the street. It was a street like any other.

"Yes, you *do*," she said angrily. "You love me."

"No," I said again, feeling as if for the rest of my life the only thing I'd be able to say was no.

"I think you do," she said.

"And what does Stresa think?" I said.

I distinctly heard her catch her breath. Then I heard her voice, cracked with pain. "Who told you?" she said in desperation.

Just then, Graziano came out of the station house. He was smiling and waving his hand as if to silence applause. "I fooled them," he said as he got in the car.

"What did you do?" I said.

"I apologized. Where shall we go to celebrate my regained freedom?"

"I'm going home," Arianna said. She was looking straight ahead in that conceited way of hers.

"Why?" Graziano said, but nobody replied, so after a moment he said, "All right, if that's the way things are," and lit a cigar.

Nobody said another word until we got to Piazza del Popolo. There, Arianna waited for us to get out, still looking straight ahead. Graziano hesitated for a moment, chewed his cigar a couple of times, then got out after me. He stood there watching the little English car disappear at the far end of the square.

"Well," he said, "it's always the best who leave."

"Let's go sit down," I said, pointing to the obelisk. The square was deserted and you could hear the noise of the fountains. We sat down with our backs to the Pincio.

"What's happening to you, Leo?" Graziano said.

"I'm tired," I said, "very tired."

"The whole world's tired," he said. "What can we do?" Then he produced the bottle of scotch from his pocket and took a big slug. He looked at it in disgust. "These pick-me-ups pick me up less and less," he said, putting the bottle back in his pocket. "What a bummer," he said, letting his gaze wander over the deserted square. "I think I'm in love with Arianna too."

8

And then came August, the black month. Under an oppressive sun, the city was deserted, the streets empty, the echoing cobbled squares covered in a layer of burning dust. Water was running low and the fountains were crumbling, showing all the signs of old age, with the cracks plastered over and tufts of yellowish grass sticking out. Cats hid in the shade of cars and only toward sunset did people start coming out of their homes to gather around the watermelon stands, waiting for the wind. According to the newspapers, it was the hottest summer in the past ten years.

As for me, it was a month I hated. With my friends gone and the trattorias closed, a person could die of starvation, with nobody to borrow money from to see him through until September. That year I had a job and the empty city shouldn't have scared me. But I was alone. I hadn't heard anything more from Arianna, Graziano must have left on his cruise, and the Diaconos had moved to their house by the sea. Sometimes I dialed their numbers anyway, just to imagine the phones ringing in their empty apartments. Apart from that, I slept until noon and then went to the pool, where I'd lie alongside it reading. There were two regulars who played chess and sometimes I challenged the winner, but the games weren't interesting. Around four, I'd go back home to rest and eat a little fruit while waiting to go to the newspaper. A couple of times I'd heard the phone ringing as I came up the stairs, but I'd never gotten to it in time. Then one afternoon it rang as I was opening the door. I lifted the receiver. It was a voice I didn't know telling me that Graziano was dead.

*The police officer on duty at the hospital got to his feet when I ar*rived and sat down again only once I'd also sat down. He was very kind. He spoke in the appropriate tone. He told me Graziano had died that morning after two days in a coma. They'd been looking for me ever since he'd been taken to the hospital because they'd found a note on him in which he'd written that whatever happened to him, they had to phone me. They'd tried several times and in the end had come to the conclusion that I was out of town. The call I'd answered was a personal attempt on the officer's part because he'd felt bad that someone could die alone like a dog. I thanked him. He said there was no need. I asked how it had happened and he said Graziano had been found by the doorman on Monday afternoon in the corner of the courtyard below his living room window. It was purely by chance, because that day the building was practically uninhabited and the doorman had gone there only to water a vacationing family's plants. The accident had happened on Sunday evening, a few hours after Graziano's wife and two daughters had left. The doorman had heard the thud but unfortunately hadn't thought anything of it because it seemed to come from another building.

So Graziano had lain there, still alive, for a night and a day on the cobblestones of the courtyard. I remembered those cobblestones, they were small and oval and grass grew in the gaps between them.

"We've been trying to get in touch with his wife for two days now," the officer said. "Do you have any idea where she could be?" I said she might be on a cruise, and he made a note of this, then asked if Graziano had any other relatives and if I knew how to get hold of them. "His father," I said, and he was about to make another note, but I told him I'd deal with it. He thanked me and asked me if I wanted to talk to the doctor, because the postmortem must be over by now. I said okay.

The officer walked ahead of me along a corridor of the hospital. The patients were leaning out the windows in search of air. It was a very hot afternoon, and the fans in the corridors were making a lot of noise but nothing else. We stopped outside a pair of double doors just long enough for the officer to take off his hat before knocking. He was a very polite policeman. "Come in," a voice said. It belonged to a male nurse sitting behind a typewriter. The doctor was at a bigger table. He was holding some papers that every now and again he used to fan his face. He must have been very hot, because he was fat, and fat people feel the heat more than thin people. He wasn't wearing a shirt under his white coat, and you could see his fat, hairless chest. "Just a minute," he said, taking off his glasses and wiping his eyes with a handkerchief. He glanced at the papers he'd been fanning himself with and resumed dictating to the nurse. The police officer motioned me to a chair and I went and sat down. "Loss of upper incisors," the doctor said to the nurse, "due to the impact. Fracture of the mandible and the third cervical vertebra, contusion with extensive hematoma on the left clavicle. Sagging of the torso with fracture of the third and fifth left rib. Death followed hemorrhage of the cerebellum. Cause: Fall." He looked at us. "Incredible," he said, "no fracture of the hands. Usually, people try to shield their face and they break their hands. This one didn't." The police officer told him who I was and the doctor looked embarrassed and invited me to sit down, even though I was already sitting. "Do you want to see him?" he said.

I didn't say anything and the doctor signaled to the nurse, who stood up from the table. I also stood up. Before leaving me, the police officer asked if I would see about the funeral and I said yes. Then I followed the nurse into the corridor with the patients at the windows. At the end of the corridor was a staircase that led to a sun-drenched courtyard full of parked cars and we made our way through them with some difficulty until we came to the door of a low, ivy-covered building. Inside, it was cold, or so it seemed to me after crossing that sunny courtyard. The door led straight into a very large room. Sheets lay in the corners, heaped up any old way. There was a single table, right in the middle, with something on it wrapped in a sheet. I went closer. On the floor were dark patches of something I assumed was blood, which suggested they'd dragged Graziano in order to get him on the table.

Graziano was there, in the sheet. His face was uncovered, and also part of his chest, protruding in a ghastly way. All the parts of him that could be seen were swollen. For a moment it crossed my mind that this was all a mistake, that it wasn't him, that he was on a cruise, as he was supposed to be. He was hard to recognize at first because they'd scraped back his hair, revealing his forehead, but then I recognized the curve of his nose and his thin, motionless lips, and then the two hunger scars on his stomach. I felt like crying, but I didn't. I was aware of the nurse waiting at the door and would have liked to tell him to leave, but I didn't feel like speaking. So I reached out a hand to the sheet and shifted Graziano's legs. They were colder, under the sheet, than the air in the room. When I'd made enough space for myself, I sat down on the marble table.

"You can't do that," the nurse said. I looked at him. He was small and thin. He was about to say something, but then just raised his hand and went outside.

I was glad to be alone. The cold of the marble was pleasant, and I lit a cigarette, looking at Graziano.

"Who is it?" I said when I heard the door open again.

A monk with a big purple cross on his chest came forward, moving between the sheets heaped up on the floor. "Come down off there, my son," he said, putting a hand on my arm. His beard smelled of wax. *Which floor is God on?* I took my arm away from his hand. I kept my head down so as not to look him in the face, and the smoke from my cigarette got in my eyes. "Why don't you try to pray?" the monk said.

"I don't pray," I said. "At most I say please."

He stood there looking at me with his hands clasped over his belly, then he shook his head and walked out. In the silence, I heard a fly buzzing. It must have come in when the monk opened the door. It flew around a few times and came to rest on my hand. I brushed it away and it landed on Graziano's chest. Again, I chased it away, but it came back immediately, landing on his lips this time. So I got down off the table, covered his face with the sheet, and left.

The old Alfa Romeo was scorching hot and I had to lean forward in my seat as I drove in order to avoid burning my back. At Graziano's, the doorman was there. He was mortified. He couldn't forgive himself for not going to see when he heard the noise. "I didn't even know he was home," he said. "I thought he'd left with the signora." I had him give me the keys and went up to the second floor. I had to try the whole bunch before I found the right one. Inside, the only window now open in the apartment was the bedroom window. It looked out onto the courtyard and I didn't go near it. I started searching everywhere until under the Ping-Pong table in the entranceway I found his notebook with the telephone numbers. I went through it without finding his father's number, he probably knew it by heart or maybe he never phoned him. Instead, I found the numbers of a few people I also knew, most of them by sight, and those of a few mutual friends. Mine was there too. I called all of them on the phone in the living room, but not a single person was home. Then I put the notebook in my pocket and went to the newspaper.

"How come you're so early?" Rosario said. "Did something happen?"

"No," I said, "nothing."

I took out the Florence phone books and called all the Castelvecchios I could find, but none of those who answered had any connection with Graziano. I made a mark with my pen next to those numbers that didn't answer so that I could try them again later and told Rosario he could go. I wanted to get straight down to work, but as soon as he was gone I realized I'd made a mistake. I was too tired to put up with our correspondents' inanities, but it was too late now, so I started to answer the calls. Every time I finished transcribing an article I tried to call Florence.

Around midnight I got hold of Graziano's father. He was a taxi driver and had been on his shift until eleven. Although he had an old man's voice, it wasn't so unlike his son's. He listened in silence to what I had to tell him and remained silent even when I'd finished. When he spoke again, he was crying. He said he would leave right away, he would inform the garage and leave right away, but I told him he didn't have to leave until the following morning, it was better for him to rest.

It was only after talking to him that I remembered I hadn't called an undertaker. I looked in the phone book for the ones with the flashiest advertising. They were very helpful, even at that hour of the night, and assured me they'd go to the hospital and get everything ready in time.

I didn't have anything else to do. The phones were quiet. So I went to the window to smoke and look at the deserted street and the streetlights. Every now and again a car passed, breaking the silence of the night. Then, with indescribable slowness, the sky started to lighten until it was time to go home.

The funeral was the next day. All morning I stayed by the phone with Graziano's notebook in my hand but couldn't get hold of anyone to inform and in the end gave up. His father arrived around noon in his taxicab. He was a pale, nervous little man, his eyes red from tears. He immediately wanted to see his son and I left him alone in the morgue and waited for him in the courtyard. There were cats roaming between the parked cars.

A man came forward into the sun, mopping his forehead with a handkerchief. He was from the undertaker's. He said they couldn't use the suit Graziano had died in because of the bloodstains. He asked if they should buy one. I said no and went to Graziano's apartment. There was a closet full of suits. I took out a white one and went back to the hospital, where I handed it over to the still-sweating man. Then I went and sat down next to Graziano's father on a granite bench against the ivy-covered wall. He was staring at the cats among the cars. "He didn't have any ideals," he said. "You can't live without ideals." I noticed that he was wearing a war invalid's silver badge in his buttonhole and I didn't say anything. This was the man we'd killed in our story, an old man.

We sat waiting in silence and after a while the police officer I already knew showed up. He apologized and handed me a sheet of paper and an envelope with the things Graziano had in his pocket when he'd been brought into the hospital. There were a bunch of keys, a wad of money, an initialed silk handkerchief, a cigar butt, and a wilted carnation that for some reason reminded me of Sant'Elia, maybe because the stalk was cut just the right length to be inserted in a buttonhole. I signed the paper and gave everything to Graziano's father, except the carnation, which I put in my pocket.

The man from the undertaker's came to tell us that everything was ready. We followed him into the chapel of rest. There was an intolerable scent coming from a few bunches of flowers and an electric fan was humming, pointing straight at Graziano, stirring the collar of his shirt. "He doesn't have shoes," I said and the man from the undertaker's said he hadn't been wearing any but that they could send someone to buy a pair. This time too I said no. I didn't like keeping them waiting, but I took the old Alfa Romeo and went back to the apartment. After I found the shoes, I set off in search of a smoke shop. It wasn't easy to find one that was open. I drove back with the shoes and the cigarettes.

Graziano's father was again sitting in the shade of the ivy. I gave the shoes to the man from the undertaker's, who had to struggle to get them on the feet. I turned away until he'd done it. "Can we close it up?" he said, and I put the pack of Lucky Strikes in the coffin.

"Close it up," I said, thinking he should have asked Graziano's father, but the old man sat there motionless, incapable of saying a word, and when I looked at him he merely nodded.

Three young guys in T-shirts came in with an acetylene torch and set to work. The flame was noisy and smelly and I preferred to go out into the courtyard.

It wasn't far from the hospital to the church. Graziano's father was in no shape to drive his taxi, so I got behind the wheel and followed the undertaker's van. I didn't go into the church for the service, which in any case was very short. Instead, I sat down on the rim of a dry, cracked fountain. Here too there were cats, crouching in its shade. I was joined by the man from the undertaker's. "Incredible heat," he said. "We have to be very quick in these cases. I know now's not the time," he went on, "but about the expenses . . ." I told him I'd see to it and to contact me at the *Corriere dello Sport*. He said that was fine, and went and leaned against the van.

After a while, the coffin came out of the church. Graziano's father must have been feeling bad, because two of the guys in T-shirts were supporting him. He sat down in the backseat of the taxi. He was very pale. "I haven't slept all night," he said. "And the drive didn't help," he went on. I got behind the wheel. It was a long ride to the cemetery, but the streets were empty in the sun and the van made good time. Once, it jumped a red light, but there really wasn't anybody on the streets.

It was cooler at the cemetery, but the smell of flowers wilting in the heat was suffocating. The marble headstones looked like gigantic cuttlefish bones abandoned on a beach. A priest, along with two seminarians, blessed the coffin as it descended into the grave. I wondered why the two boys were in the city, doing this crummy job, instead of being on vacation like everyone else.

When the coffin was all the way down, the priest opened his book, but I told him no and took out *The Last of the Mohicans*. I hadn't even needed to mark the page, the last sentences were what I wanted to read. I approached the sun-filled grave while Graziano's father went and leaned against a cart full of dried-out flowers. "'Why do my brothers mourn?' he said," I read aloud, "*regarding the dark race of dejected warriors by whom he was environed; 'why do my daughters weep? that a young man has gone to the happy hunting-grounds; that a chief has filled his time with honor? He was good; he was dutiful; he was brave. Who can deny it? The Manitou had need of such a warrior, and He has called him away. As for me, the son and the father of Uncas, I am a blazed pine, in a clearing of the pale faces. My race has gone from the shores of the salt lake and the hills of the Delawares. But who can say that the serpent of his tribe has forgotten his wisdom?*'" Then I closed the book and left.

The avenue in front of the cemetery was deserted. I looked over toward the bus stop, because my old Alfa Romeo was still outside the hospital and I had to go pick it up, but I couldn't make up my mind to move. It struck me as impossible that I couldn't do anything else for Graziano. But there really was nothing more I could do for him. Nothing at all.

By the middle of August the swallows had gone. They'd never before left so early and when I went out on the balcony in the evening to wait for the wind, the sky was empty and silent. The newspapers claimed the birds had gone because of the poisoned air that hung over the city, but that was a childish explanation. The truth is, the higher you go, the better you can see things.

I didn't read, didn't go to the movies, didn't do anything. I spent my days waiting to go to the newspaper office. The one thing I was proud of, the one thing that kept me going, was that I wasn't drinking. I'd even bought a bottle of Ballantine's and kept it in full view on the table without touching it. Then, ten days before the beginning of September, I received a letter from Arianna. *Dear darling Leo. Hey, where are you? What are you doing?* Who with? *Not hearing anything from you worries me. Everyone's really nice to me here, but I've been through some rough patches. I kept waking up at night, afraid I was suffocating, and wanted desperately to go back to the clinic. For the whole of the first week, Eva bombarded Livio with phone calls. Then she came. There was an unpleasant scene, at the end of which they went off together. To hell with the two of them. I'm fine now. All I do is eat, I'm afraid I'll get very fat. But I also swim, and I go on wonderful excursions out to sea on board a lovely boat. I've discovered I'm crazy about boats. Today it's raining, though, and I'm sad. I'm aware of how alone I am in the middle of this vast, terrible world. I don't know where to go. What will I do with my life? Why don't you get the hell out of there and come fetch me? I beg you, I beg you, I beg you.*

There was a return address, and two days later I asked the paper for time off and set out in my car. I didn't take the highway—the best thing of all about highways is that they leave normal roads clear. The old Alfa Romeo thundered as it climbed the slopes of the Castelli Romani, surrounded by a landscape that was wild and arid but already taking on the first faint colors of fall. Once past the Castelli, a long descent began, and at last, after a very long, straight road lined with plane trees, the sea appeared. I drove without hurrying in the noonday sun. The farther south I drove, the more magnificent the coast became. The road, wide and direct, ran across bare, stony mountains, sometimes high above the sea that glittered below in little rocky inlets, sometimes dipping to run alongside beaches that were white and deserted. Then the Saracen towers appeared, hanging sheer over the sea. And it was at this point that I saw the bay.

It was wider than the others, and you could see for kilometers along the two blue arms of land that extended into the sea. Low undergrowth separated the beach from the road, and on a rocky promontory a dark Saracen fortress rose in the sun. I stopped the car and stripped off my clothes, then walked barefoot into the undergrowth until I found a gap leading to the beach. The sand was scorching hot, but the water was cool and clean. I dove in and swam until I was out of breath. Then I turned on my back and played dead, listening to the swish of the water around my ears. I felt good, I couldn't remember ever feeling that good. Then I turned back to the shore, swimming calmly in the direction of the mountains.

I dried myself in the sun, then got back in my car and set off again. I drove barefoot, and as the water dried it left a layer of salt on my skin. When I felt hungry I stopped to have some fish at a roadside trattoria. Resuming my journey, I started asking for information in all the built-up areas I passed through. Finally, a young boy said he knew the villa I was looking for and offered to show me the way for a thousand lire.

The villa had been built around a Saracen tower and was low and very white, shaded by maritime pines and oleander bushes.

In front of the gate there were some sports cars and some official-looking cars. I left the old Alfa Romeo there, although it was neither a sports car nor an official car, and pulled on a small chain that stuck out of the wall next to the gate. A bell rang in the distance, followed by the barking of dogs.

After five minutes a butler in a white jacket appeared. "There's nobody home," he said. "They're all out boating. The master's in his studio but can't be disturbed."

"Giacomo, who is it?" a voice cried from the tower.

"It's for the signorina!" Giacomo yelled back, and then the voice shouted that I should make myself at home.

The butler led me along a concrete path to a terrace overlooking the sea. It was full of white chairs adorned with arabesques and brightly colored cushions. "Would you like a tall drink?" the servant said. I was still drinking it when a quarter of an hour later the host appeared. I knew him, it was the second time I'd seen him. His name was Arlorio and his paintings—seascapes, sailboats, freight cars, harlequins—filled the drawing rooms of half of Rome. He was as tall as I remembered him, lean, with a semi-halo of gray hair around his sinewy neck. He looked like Picasso, only taller and harder, and without Picasso's luminous smile. "They're all on the boat," he said. "You'll have to wait for them."

"That's okay," I said.

He had bright, quick eyes, like a bird of prey's, and long, sinewy, probing fingers. He was sunburned, and was wearing only a skimpy swimsuit with white and red flowers on it. His knees bore the marks of old wounds, those unmistakable scars left by childhood battles. I was surprised that someone like him could ever have been a child. When he sat down he pinched his thighs, the gesture of someone who's not used to sitting down without his pants on. If I'd wanted to, I would have laughed. "What was the weather like in Rome?" he said.

"August."

"I know what you mean," he said. "Very hot. I don't know why Arianna wants to go back. She's so unpredictable," he said, choosing just the right adjective. "I assume you're great friends. Is that right?"

"Yes, it is."

"Just friends?" he said. I looked him in the eyes, and he laughed, if only halfheartedly. "She told me you're a journalist. At the *Corriere dello Sport*, I think. Do you like it?" he said hurriedly, "because I have lots of friends who are journalists and I think I could do something for you."

"I like it a lot."

"Better that way," he said, opening his hands wide. Then he looked around. "Better that way," he said again. "Would you like a drink?" I said no, and he smiled. Then he excused himself, saying he still had a little work to do but that I should make myself at home. If I wanted to take a dip, I just had to ask Giacomo for a swimsuit. Besides, the others shouldn't be much longer. Anyway, he really had to go. He apologized again and walked away, whistling for the dogs. Soon afterward, the music of a Bach chorale wafted down from the tower.

It was four when a throbbing came from the sea. A boat appeared, gradually revealing itself as a large cabin cruiser. It moored at the jetty below the cliff and a few people disembarked, all in the same white and red flowered swimsuits. Among them was Arianna, her hair hanging loose on her shoulders. Her harmonious, touchingly girlish body was dark and shiny. She looked very happy. I heard her voice as they climbed the steps carved into the rock. She was saying something about how tired she was, and a blond young man wearing a necklace of shells put an arm around her shoulders. They vanished into the coastal vegetation and when they reappeared their voices were very close. All at once, they were on the terrace.

Arianna was amazed to see me. "My God! It's over! It's over!" she cried theatrically and kissed me on the cheek. "How's Graziano?" she said.

"Fine."

"What a fucked-up son of a bitch," she said. "Not even a postcard. But what are you wearing?" she went on, looking at my khaki pants. "Didn't you have a pair of jeans? Come on, let me introduce you to the others. Have you already met Mauro?" she said, referring to Arlorio. I shook several hands. Everyone was very casual and tanned. Just then Arlorio appeared at the top of the tower and made a broad gesture as if blessing them. "*Introibo ad altare Dei.*" Christ! Everyone laughed, but Arianna's face turned serious for a fraction of a second. Then she took me by the hand and smiled. "You already know each other, I *assume*?" she said in her conceited way. Arlorio nodded gravely and blessed me too. "I have to pack," she said. "Will you come with me to my room?" We went back along part of the concrete path, between the oleanders, then turned onto another path that was very short and led to a room isolated from the rest of the house. It had a large window that looked out on the sea and was filled with light. The furniture consisted of a table, an antique pier glass, and a bed covered in the same white-and-red-flowered material as the swimsuits.

I watched Arianna as she filled a suitcase in silence. She acted as if I wasn't there, and when she took off her swimsuit, I felt humiliated. Not bothering with panties, she put on a very threadbare pair of jeans and a transparent lace blouse and red rubber sandals on her feet. "I'm ready," she said.

We went back to the terrace. They were all lying on white chairs and when they saw us they raised a chorus of protests. "What a bore you are!" one girl said. "Couldn't you have left with us on Sunday?" Arlorio, leaning on the parapet that overhung the cliff, smiled and said we should both stay until Sunday. Arianna glared at him, then started saying good-bye to the others. That took a while, as it involved making appointments for when she would be in Rome. The last person she said good-bye to was Arlorio. He was still smiling, which irritated her. "Bye," she said to him. Then she turned because the servant had appeared with her suitcase. "Shall we get the hell out of here?" she said to me and set off. We'd reached the end of the terrace when we heard Arlorio's voice again. "Arianna!" he called. "Aren't you forgetting something?"

"*What*, according to you?"

"You know perfectly well," Arlorio said, holding out a hand.

For a moment, Arianna stared at him with her big eyes, then started searching in the pockets of her jeans. They were very tight and she had to struggle to pull out the pack of cards. She handed it to the servant, who in turn carried it to Arlorio. He took it, weighed it in his hand, and, still smiling, threw it over his shoulder, sending it sailing down the cliff. Then even Arianna smiled.

We followed the servant in silence. When we reached the old Alfa Romeo, I went ahead of him and opened the trunk. The servant put in the suitcase and then dusted off his hands. "Good-bye, signorina," he said. "I hope to see you again in Rome." Arianna nodded and got in the car.

For the first hundred kilometers neither of us spoke. Arianna was silent, looking out the window at the stony mountains as they faded in the sunset. The sea was taking on the color of pearls. There was great sadness in the speed at which the days were getting shorter. As if they were trying to redeem something that was irredeemable. With a sense of heartache, I thought about September, when the ferocity of summer would abate.

"Why did you want me to come and get you?" I said.

She didn't reply immediately. Then she said, "You're right, I'm sorry."

I knew perfectly well why she'd done it. She'd wanted to show me off to Arlorio just as she'd shown him off to me that evening outside the gates of Sant'Elia's villa. Arlorio's advantage was that he didn't know. But, then, I guess he had all the advantages. For me, it was over.

The road was running alongside the railroad tracks now. It was getting dark. In the dark it wasn't too difficult to keep quiet. The straight, tree-lined road was full of shadows and the wind came in cool through the windows. We came to the lights of the first little town on the Castelli, where we stopped at a trattoria and had a quick bite. Then we left again immediately and within an hour we were on the outskirts of Rome.

"Shall I drive you home?" I said, but she said she was never going back to Eva's. "Where, then?"

"I don't know," she said. "I thought your place. For a few days."

"No," I said.

"You figured it all out, didn't you?" she said, trying to smile.

The city was coming back to life. More and more people were returning every day and somehow everything would go back to being the way it was before. Nothing ever changed in this city, that's the way it was.

I said I'd take her to a hotel.

"All right," she said, searching in her handbag for something. The car filled with the scent of lilac. "Forgive me," she said. "I'm really sorry."

9

I was drunk from morning to night. Just like the good old days, truth be told. The days drifted by and summer had turned to fall and fall was turning to winter. The only god-awful moment was waking. Throwing up in the morning is one of the most unpleasant aspects of a period of intense alcoholic activity, but apart from that I couldn't complain. I kept going to the newspaper office, even when I could barely type because my hands were shaking so much. My fingers would get stuck between the keys and my nails were constantly broken. Most of the time I sat there in front of the typewriter while the disc turned and turned. When the girls got tired of having to do my work for me, they tipped off the head of the department. The pit bull came over all understanding at first, then, getting nowhere with that, conveyed the message that at the end of November I would have to go. But there is a kind of justice in the world, because two days before my time was up his expired. Not that he died, only that there was some kind of revolution at the paper, which I vaguely heard about, at the end of which the head of department was dismissed and his place taken by Rosario. I'd wound up safe and sound.

In the evening, I would go to Signor Sandro's and once I'd gotten on top of the situation I would go outside and fight with the police. People in uniform had always bothered me and when I drank I felt an absolute necessity to tell them that. I picked on anyone in uniform, even streetcar drivers, but apart from police officers my favorites were hotel doormen.

I would get home exhausted. In the morning, if I could manage to stand on my feet, I'd take the movie script and do the rounds of the film companies. I wasn't doing it only for Graziano but for me. I was still paying his funeral expenses, which had been astronomical. But nothing came of it. I rarely managed to speak with anyone more important than a secretary—I even ended up in bed with a couple of them, I think. Then one day I actually got to see a producer.

He was young, dynamic, northern, and penniless. He'd read the script and liked it a lot. There was someone else with him in the office, a guy in jeans and sweater, a director. I'd seen some of his movies, Westerns that weren't as bad as you might have thought, given the titles, and we spoke affably. He liked the project, he said, even though the screenplay would have to be changed in ways that wouldn't affect the basic story. A lot depended on the price, the producer said rather warily. I said that wouldn't be a problem, they seemed relieved, and the tone became affable again. They even had the right actor available, a young pop singer who was making a name for himself in movies. True, he was a little young, but one of the director's ideas was to reduce the age of the main character by about ten years. "I'd make him one of those long-haired young guys from a good family," he said, "a young pacifist. The fact that he kills his father becomes much more emblematic."

"Maybe he should play the flute on Piazza Navona," I said. The director half closed his eyes, weighing up the idea. He thought it was a good one.

We talked some more, ever more affably as the bottle of whisky on the table gradually emptied. When it was finished, I pushed it across the table and told them where they could stick it and why. They were very upset by that, and even tried to grab hold of me, but I brandished the bottle and managed to get the hell out of there unscathed. I still had the bottle in my hand when I hit the street, so I headed to the nearest bar. They refused to fill it with hot water and I argued with them at length, maintaining that the bottle was glass, not plastic, and so must still have a modicum of value on the stock exchange. But they didn't understand about high finance, so I left. The first thing I saw on the street was a policeman getting out of a patrol car. I threw myself at the car door just as he was sticking his head out. I learned later that he lost two teeth.

As for me, I woke up in an iron bed as a woman's face with heavy, patient features surmounted by a white cap leaned in a few centimeters from mine. Immediately, I felt a needle piercing my arm. The syringe was full of red liquid. I saw the straps at the sides of the bed. I asked if they'd used them.

"Only the first night," the nurse said.

"How long have I been here?"

"Four days."

"Give me my clothes," I said, sitting up. We were in a large ward full of beds, but only two were occupied, one by me and one by somebody or other near the door. I wanted to see the doctor and get the hell out of there, but when I tried to stand up I felt dizzy and my knees sagged. I was freezing cold even though there were some big radiators against the cracked walls.

"I'll bring you another blanket," the nurse said as she helped me back into bed. "You can see the doctor at noon. Is there any-one you want informed that you're here?"

I didn't reply and pulled the blanket over my shoulders. I fell asleep again until the next day and when I woke I felt fine and wanted a drink. The nurse—not the same one, another one—said that as far as the drink went, I could forget it, but that if I wanted to I could speak with the doctor. That was something, at least, a doctor. I said I wanted to see him right away and then go.

By now almost all the beds in the ward were occupied. I was led to an office with a cupboard and a desk. Behind the desk was a curt old man. The first thing he said, after I'd sat down opposite him, was to ask if I wanted to die.

"No," I said.

"Then look at this," he said, holding out a sheet of paper. I didn't take it. He gave me a glance and put it down on the desk. "Do you know what sundown syndrome is?" he said. I shook my head, and he started reading aloud what was on the paper. I heard him say a whole lot of stuff about confusion, primitive personality disorders, anxiety attacks, mood swings, delirium, confabulation. I liked *confabulation* a lot. "Do you ever see mice?" he said. This one scared me. Why should I see mice? I wasn't at that point yet. I didn't say anything, but he noticed my concern and put the paper to one side. "Do you recall throwing an empty bottle at the mirror in a bar and then attacking the police? There's a report about you." All I remembered was the police officer. The doctor kept looking at me, then he dropped his pencil on the desk and delivered his verdict. "You should never touch another drop of alcohol," he said. "Your liver won't let you. You have to be careful. There are people who can drink and people who can't. You can't. Get that in your head, if you want to go on living. Otherwise, do what you like."

"I won't drink anymore," I said.

"It's up to you."

"I won't drink anymore," I said again. "Can I go now?"

"If you feel up to it," he said. I thanked him and headed for the door. As I opened it, he spoke again. "Gazzara," he said. I turned because his voice sounded different, kindlier. "It'll be hard," he said when I looked at him.

"I know," I said. "I tried once before." Suddenly, I felt like crying.

"Come back if you need help," he said.

I closed the door and headed along the corridor. A nurse was pushing a cart loaded with red syringes. It clinked like a cart full of bottles. I stopped her and asked her if I could have my clothes. I went back to the big ward and sat down on my bed and waited. When the nurse came in with my clothes, I asked her what day it was. It was ten days to Christmas.

*Whenever you quit drinking, you get the impression the world is tak-*ing the opportunity to attack you from all sides, but, in my case, it wasn't only an impression. The next day, at home, I was awakened by a kind of muffled, monotonous throbbing I'd never heard before. I went to the window and saw that the valley was done for. In the cold December sun, a digger was uprooting the trees, leaving a dark trail across the meadow like a wound. They were constructing something and as usual they were starting by destroying everything. It went on like this for days and days, and every now and again the throbbing of the digger was joined by the crack of a tree being felled, but from this point on the only time I was home was to sleep.

I could barely keep on my feet. The alcohol had gone from my veins, leaving a void I didn't know how to fill. I forced myself to eat a lot of meat and fresh vegetables, one of the recommendations on the sheet of paper I'd been given on leaving the hospital, along with some blue compresses, but all I could manage to drink, and then only with difficulty, was a little tea and some orange juice.

One day, thinking it might be easier to eat with company, I phoned the Diaconos. Viola answered, but hearing behind her voice other voices I knew I made an appointment for the following evening.

When I arrived, I walked in and there in the living room, behind the white velvet couch, was a Christmas tree not much smaller than the one in the Rinascente department store. "The city's gone crazy," Viola said. "Have you been downtown lately?"

I'd carefully avoided doing so. If there was one thing I couldn't stand, it was the decorations on the streets and the white-bearded Santas outside the stores. Even Christmas trees I'd been unable to stand, since they'd started making them out of plastic. But I didn't tell her that, not only because the Diaconos' tree was a real tree, with scent and everything, but because I was fine as I was and didn't want to talk. I watched the servant going back and forth, setting the table. There was a nice family atmosphere just then, as we waited for Renzo to get back from the TV center.

And there was something else. I'd seen colorful packages heaped up in the hallway and they'd reminded me of long-buried Christmases in Milan: the cold, damp air, the smell of fog and mandarin oranges, and especially the stores, the magnificently decorated delicatessens with their mountains of fresh cheeses, strings of sausages, delicious hot dogs. At Christmas my father would order whole baskets of provisions, and all afternoon, on Christmas Eve, errand boys would be coming and going, ringing the doorbell and unloading stacks of marvels on the kitchen table, while my sisters would shriek and start to taste a little of everything, annoying my mother because they would ruin the appearance of the dishes. God, we were actually happy once! I was seized by the sudden urge to go to Milan.

"Christmas used to be more intimate," Viola said. "Now this whole gift thing is completely crazy. Do you know how much Renzo's had to spend on gifts?"

"This is for you," my father would say, "and this is for you, and this is for you," as he distributed the gifts. He never said our names. God knows why.

"Have you heard from Arianna?"

"Why should I?" I said, a knife starting to twist inside me. "Maybe she's growing lilacs."

"Crazy stuff," Viola said. She didn't know what I was talking about, but then she hadn't been outside Sant'Elia's villa. "What's his name, that Arlorio, he's stopping her from seeing her sister, which means she can't see us either. Eva's desperate. She's in a terrible state." She looked at me. "You did know she's with Arlorio, didn't you?" she said hesitantly. I said no and she bit her lip, so I told her I'd assumed it and she recovered. She grew meditative. "Why did it end like that, Leo?" she said, but I didn't reply. Managing not to think about it was difficult enough without other people interfering. But Viola wanted to talk. "A lot of it's Eva's fault. She was absurdly jealous. I'm not even referring to Livio—that was pure madness, in my opinion—I'm referring to before, to you. She couldn't bear it that Arianna was in love with you."

That's how I found out that Arianna had been in love with me. That's how I found out, in the intimate, persuasive tones of a piece of gossip, that she'd been in love with me. There had been terrible scenes because of me. Eva couldn't understand how Arianna could be in love with a fucked-up guy like me. All they did was fight, but the most violent quarrel was when I'd run away from the TV center. They were all at dinner together, and Arianna, who was extremely anxious, kept getting up to phone me, until Eva exploded. There were smashed plates and tears and, in the end, Arianna walked out, saying she was going to live with me. But she couldn't find me and at five in the morning had gone to the Diaconos'. She was in such a state, they had to call a doctor. "She couldn't breathe," Viola said. I didn't say anything. I was thinking about the evening after that, when she came to my apartment and I turned my back on her and left her in the armchair.

Renzo walked in and gave me one of his slaps on the back. "Look who's here," he said. "What do you think of the tree?"

"He's a barbarian, as usual," Viola said with a laugh. "He hasn't given it a second glance."

They made me nauseous. I was thinking about what Viola had said as she walked me to the door the evening I'd run away from the TV center. *Phone Arianna, you know how she dramatizes*—that's what she'd said. After everything that had happened, after seeing her in that state, that's what she'd said. But that's the way they were. They took everything in stride. They were frivolous and sure of themselves. They crushed people with a one-liner and then walked on by, toward the first armchair at hand. Well, this was another place to cross off my list. I had to make an effort to talk to them over dinner. Then I had to make another effort to play chess with Renzo. I was thinking about Milan. I felt a kind of yearning for the serious, slightly dull life of my gloomy city. I was tired of one-liners and social gatherings where you killed people coldly, without drawing blood, as if they were clothes you could discard.

When I left, an icy wind, the kind that cuts your hands, was wiping the city clean, and above it was a sky that could break your heart. I raised the collar of my coat and got in the old Alfa Romeo. Sheltered from the wind, I counted what money I had. It was enough. There was a train at one, and I just had time to catch it. I traveled all night.

The train was packed, and you couldn't breathe in the compartment. So I went out into the corridor and sat down on a stool, resting my forehead against the window. It wasn't comfortable, but I fell asleep listening to the voices that came from the dark-shrouded compartments. The last thing I heard was a girl laughing, in the silence of some small station, then I didn't hear anything more, and didn't feel anything either, not even the cold of the window on my forehead.

I woke twice. Once was in the middle of the night as the train crossed the Apennines. They were covered in snow, and I sat looking at them and smoking a cigarette. The second time was when it was almost dawn and we were speeding across the Po Valley. Two hours later I was in Milan.

I got off the train into a grim morning. I was at the end of my tether and I could smell that railroad smell on me that you're always left with after spending the night on a train. I couldn't show up at home in this state, without even a suitcase. I went to the public baths. The face I saw in the mirror made me realize what a desperate undertaking this was. It was my eyes that betrayed me. They were swollen and red and my cheeks were hollow and flaccid like an old man's. I took a shower and got a haircut, but it didn't greatly improve my appearance. Then I tried having breakfast, but the coffee was disgusting and scorching hot, the plastic-wrapped brioche seemed straight out of a tire factory, and the barista was not much more than a dishwasher who did everything in a hurry. I had to make an effort not to get back on a train and leave.

I knew the smell of the air, that smell of fog and smoking brushwood that Milan always has in winter. It had snowed the day before and the sidewalks were lined with heaps of dirty, frozen snow. The buildings rose in a light haze that muffled sounds, every now and again brightened by a sun that seemed about to be snuffed out. It was cold.

I was still stiff when I got on a streetcar—*the streetcars there are great*—and sat down on one of the smooth, shiny wooden benches. Around me, people were talking in that old, forgotten accent. They were pale and drained, ready for the daily carnage.

I began to recognize the streets of my neighborhood. There

were many new stores since I'd lived there and it was pretty much from the names only that I recognized the streets. That morning I noticed the changes with greater clarity than before, and yet some things reemerged from the past—an osteria with a green sign of a ballerina in a white tutu, the stores run by the Chinese, the tobacconist's where the hookers went to have a chat and brush their hair—all things that were still standing, huddled between new stores with plate glass windows.

Then all of a sudden I didn't recognize anything anymore. Where was that ugly Baroque church? For a moment I thought the streetcar had changed route and instinctively I checked the names of the streets. They were the right ones, but the church wasn't there, and not only the church, as I could see when I got off the streetcar, but even the hill facing our apartment building. It had been a wooded hill, with granite steps and long slopes down which as a boy I'd slid during long, icy winters, once breaking my arm. It wasn't there anymore. It had been flattened and in its place was a low, covered market. But that wasn't what astonished me most. It was the fact that it had all happened so quickly, in not much more than a year.

I got off the streetcar and started wandering around the market. It was overflowing with merchandise, especially fruit and fir trees heaped up in the corners, spreading an absurd forest smell. I bought a bunch of grapes and started eating them. They were so cold they set my teeth on edge. As I ate, I looked at my home. It was the same as ever, but it still didn't arouse any emotion in me. It was the street that ruined everything. It had been a clean street once, but now it made me sick to my stomach. I finished the grapes, including the stalk, and made to cross over to the building but stopped.

My father was coming out the front door. I was about to call to him, then I thought I'd follow him and slip my hand under his arm, as if it was the most normal thing in the world, and see the look of surprise on his face, but I didn't move. In appearance, he hadn't changed, his body was big inside his coat, his stride still soft and imposing, but I knew that if I looked in his eyes, I would see how much he'd aged. I stood there, not moving, while he walked to his car. He opened the car door, then looked back toward the building. I followed the direction of his gaze and saw my mother at the window. He gestured to her with his hand, a wave that was also an admonition to go back inside so she wouldn't catch cold, but she didn't move, just smiled and gestured in return, telling him to go. It was a ritual I'd never seen them perform. Maybe it had started when they'd been left on their own. My father got in the car and sat for a while, waiting for the engine to warm up, with that incredible respect he had for inanimate things. All the while, my mother stayed at the window, but it was closed now, so I couldn't see her well, couldn't see how she was. When at last the car set off, wheezing toward the intersection, my mother disappeared from the window.

I still didn't move. I'd never seen them looking so calm. Of course, they weren't thinking about me, so why should I bother them? It was two days before Christmas and everything must have been organized already for lunch with their daughters, their daughters' husbands, and their daughters' children. All good people, but what did I have in common with them? I could already hear my mother's questions, see my father's silent looks, hear my sisters' comments from the height of the compact little mound of respectability on which they'd built their nests. I'd left so long ago, why should I disturb them at Christmas, of all times?

Anyway, I had to do something, at least move. It was too cold to just stand there. So I went in search of a delicatessen and wandered around until I found one that was okay. Inside, it was more lush and more resplendent than a cathedral. I ordered a hot dog with extra sauerkraut and a little mustard and ate it as I headed back to the train station on foot. The hot dog was excellent, well worth a trip to Milan, truth be told.

It was strange, but I didn't even feel sad. Not too sad, at least. A little bit fucked-up, that's for sure. After a while, I caught the streetcar. With luck, I might find a good book at the station kiosk and a train that wasn't too crowded. And I *was* lucky. The book was good, and the train practically empty. The sadness only hit me when the train pulled out and I realized that if it had headed in another direction, any direction, it would have been all the same to me.

At the end of January I received a letter from Glauco and Serena. It was the first one in two years and as soon as I saw it I also knew it would be the last. They were coming back. They told me the day and the number of their flight and I thought I should go to meet them. I spent two days tidying the apartment. I had to get help from the doorman, because there were lots of diggers in the valley now and they were raising a god-awful amount of dust. For months I'd been neglecting the place and there was a lot to do before the three rooms began to look decent.

I realized they'd changed as soon as I saw them getting off the plane. I had difficulty in distinguishing them from the other passengers, then I recognized Glauco's boxer's stride and, next to him, the slim figure of Serena under a poncho. They waved their arms as they came toward me. Glauco was the first to reach me. He'd put on weight and was much jollier than when he'd left. He must have gotten his heavyweight title back. He shook my hand warmly. Serena, though, kissed me on the lips. "Don't look at me," she said, "it's been a terrible flight." Actually, she looked just fine, and when she saw the old Alfa Romeo she laughed. "You still have that old thing?" she said. "How softhearted you are!"

We put the suitcases in the backseat and the three of us squeezed into the front. Glauco was the most contented. He'd had two shows in the best galleries in Mexico City. As for Serena, there wasn't a critic who hadn't been crazy about her set designs for *Andrea Chenier* and *Traviata*. Did I know what they'd been called? The "two brilliant Italians," that's what they'd been called. And I had no idea of the money they'd made. Numbers that would blow me away, with all those military men and those politicians. True, Glauco had been spat on by a student, but they'd learned to care less about protesters. It wasn't even clear what those people were trying to say. All they were good at was getting themselves shot down on the streets.

"Anyway," Serena said, "we made a whole lot of money and we can't wait to go back. How are things here?"

"Much the same," I said.

"How can you bear to live here?" Glauco said. "We're going back as soon as we can. Right, darling?"

They hardly noticed how tidy I'd made the apartment, and it didn't stay tidy for long after their suitcases started an avalanche. Serena extracted a Mexican nightgown from her suitcase, took a shower, and sat down on the couch to drink a bottle of tequila bought at the duty-free store.

"There's nothing like tequila," she said, "it's *fuego*! So, are you going to tell us about you or not?"

"Much the same," I said. "No, I don't drink."

"Of course, you can stay here as long as you like. You look a bit exhausted."

"He can stay forever if he wants," Glauco said, coming in from the bathroom in shorts. "It's not like you'll want to go on living here." But he didn't say anything about the concrete skeleton that had taken the place of the trees in the valley.

"I'm going back to the hotel," I said. "I've already notified them. They're giving me my old room. But tomorrow, if you don't mind."

They didn't, and, after a last drink, they started unpacking their suitcases and putting their clothes away in the closet in the bedroom. Each thing they took out had a story and they insisted on telling me every single one.

"This is for you," Serena said, giving me a small bronze totem. "It's the god of fertility." It was squat and surly, with two red stones for eyes.

"You old lecher," Glauco said, sitting down on the bed. "God knows how many girls you've had in my bed. What is it with you and women? I've never understood why they had such a weakness for you. And what about your friends?"

"Graziano died," I said.

"Oh, Christ, what are you saying?" he said. "I'm sorry. He was one of us."

Of course. I was about to tell Glauco what I thought of him when Serena came in holding the red robe. "Have you kept this rag?" she said. "Why didn't you throw it away?" She kissed me on the lips. I really couldn't stand the two of them and I was sorry I'd told them the hotel room wouldn't be ready until the next day, but there was the matter of my books and clothes to sort out and one way or another I needed an extra day. Just so as not to spend any more time with them, I went to the newspaper office even though it was my day off.

When I got back in the evening, they were watching TV. They'd had it repaired that same afternoon. I sat with them long enough to have a smoke, then went to my room. For the first time I closed the door. It took me ages to get to sleep, because ever since I'd stopped drinking I'd suffered from insomnia. I heard them moving around the apartment, between the bathroom and the hallway, and for a few minutes I also heard their voices, with Serena laughing and Glauco calling her an idiot. Then they closed their bedroom door. After a while I heard the bedsprings creaking. I switched on the lamp and started reading. When Serena went to the bathroom, she must have noticed the light filtering from under my door because I heard her laugh.

The next morning Glauco left early to look for a studio to rent and Serena brought me my coffee in bed. She was wearing the red robe, open at the chest.

"Make room," she said, sitting down on the bed while I was drinking coffee. "Why did you keep it?" she said, touching the hem of the robe.

"I thought you'd still need it."

"This rag?" she said, laughing. Then she stroked the blanket. "You don't look rested," she said.

"I haven't slept much," I said.

"Neither have I," she said.

"It must have been the flight," I said, thinking about the time, two years earlier, when I'd kissed her surrounded by suitcases.

"You could say that," she said, laughing. Then I told her I had to finish getting my books together, making it clear I thought she should get the hell out. She was shocked for a moment, then shrugged and laughed again. "Strange," she said. "You were always the strangest of Glauco's friends."

When I was alone, I peered into my cup. There was still a little coffee left and I finished it. Then I stretched out again on the bed and lay there listening to the noise of the diggers.

10

Of all the hotels I'd lived in, the one behind Campo de' Fiori was my favorite. I liked going back there in the evening, walking through the side streets and across the empty, silent squares. It was the old stone heart of the city that visionary architects had built five centuries earlier on the orders of stern pontiffs, where a disproportionate number of churches, hemmed in by houses, lifted their travertine summits to indicate the possible cruelty of heaven. By day, the area was an ants' nest, but toward evening you became aware that you were below the level of the river and on the walls of the houses stone plaques with dates on them bore witness to the levels reached by long-ago floods. Sheltered by higher embankments, the area had dried out, as it were. Large cracks furrowed the walls of the palaces, the plaster was coming away, and when you walked the streets and peered in through the windows you could see the decorated ceilings falling to pieces. The artisans in their workshops always looked as if they were repairing something.

I was seeing a lot of a girl named Sandra. She was twenty-two, and we'd meet on Piazza Navona, have dinner, and catch a movie.

She loved the art houses, but they were always showing movies I'd already seen and when eventually I told her to choose between me and the art houses she chose the art houses. Apart from that, I went to the newspaper office every day, though I wasn't working with Rosario anymore. An article I'd written, substituting for a sick journalist, had opened the doors of the newsroom to me. I couldn't think of any reason not to accept, but Rosario took it badly because I was doing what he'd always dreamed of doing and earning more than him. I was sad that he'd grown cold toward me because he'd helped me a lot in the hard times, and I tried to go see him as often as possible in the copy department but that just irritated him even more and in the end I stopped bothering.

In the spring, our tennis writer published an interview with Livio Stresa. He was playing tournaments again and the journalist wondered if at the age of forty and after such a long period of inactivity he was still capable of good things. The tournament was being held in Rome and I followed it in the articles we published. To everyone's surprise, Stresa played some great matches and was lucky enough to get to the finals, where he'd be playing against a twenty-year-old Pole who'd just defeated the top seed. I thought about it for a while, then decided to go see the match.

It was a gorgeous spring day and in the stands there were movie actors, directors, writers, journalists, the most beautiful girls in the city, and those women whose pictures you usually saw in the glossy magazines. There was a great sense of anticipation and everyone was rushing to grab the best seats. I looked for the group in the center stands, where the most expensive seats were, but didn't see them. Instead, I spotted them on the lower stands at the far end of the court, where you could watch the match without moving your head and root for your favorite just a few meters from the backs of the players. They were all there, wearing strange little white hats—the Diaconos, Eva, the young Russian, the model, the humorist, and the writer with the white mustache, who had published a book in the winter that hadn't won a major prize. Only Arianna was missing. When Stresa came out onto the court the whole group got to its feet and yelled, but he was very nervous and barely looked at them.

It was a long, brutal match. Stresa was a good player, cool and intelligent, while the Pole, who was blond and much appreciated by the ladies, played with real passion. It was immediately clear that the winner would be whoever was best able to withstand the pressure.

For almost three hours the group swung between excitement and despondency. Whenever Stresa played on that side of the court, they cheered so much that several times the line umpire had to ask for silence. It was definitely a nail-biter, and when at the beginning of the fifth set Stresa started to shoot his backhand into the net I also cheered him on. I don't know why I did. Maybe because I was cured, maybe because he was suffering in that subtle, cruel way made up of silence and solitude in which tennis can make people suffer, maybe because I'd seen him handing a glass to Eva in the lobby of a theater, and because now, down there, in the middle of all these people yelling, he no longer looked like a disorientated bird but like a fighting cock with bloodied spurs. Or maybe because both of us once had Arianna in our arms and lost her.

The last set was played in a nervous hush as the two players exchanged deadly volleys. On a drop shot of Stresa's, the Pole made a last leap and caught the ball under the net, lifting it just enough to put it back in play. I saw Stresa standing motionless at the other end of the court, his eyes closed. A cry went up. I recognized Eva's voice. Then, from the stands, applause erupted as if at last everyone had been set free. The Pole's nerves gave out all at once and he burst into copious tears. Stresa managed to smile and put an arm around his opponent's neck to congratulate him. I was pleased I'd cheered him on. I'd always liked good losers.

I headed for the exit, through the crowd. I was almost at the gates when I heard someone call my name. It was Eva. She must have lost the rest of the group, because she was alone.

"What are you doing?" she said hesitantly. "Aren't you going to say hello?" Then we were pushed back toward the stands and she had to grab hold of my arm. "God, what horrible people!" she said, frightened. Her face was red from the sun and her dark glasses reflected the crowd around us.

"I didn't see you," I said. "I feel sorry for Livio, he played a great game."

But it wasn't Stresa she wanted to talk about. The crowds scared her and she kept looking around nervously. "Have you heard from Arianna?" she asked, without letting go of my arm. "Did you know that man doesn't want me to see her? Did you know she hates me? I really hoped I'd see her today!"

I too looked around. I saw some of the group. The crowd had scattered them and they were searching for one another, calling out one another's names.

Eva wouldn't let go of my arm. "Are you sure you haven't heard from her? *I beg you!* Tell me if you know something," she said with a moan, as the multitude struggled on the surface of her glasses.

"No," I said, "I don't know anything. If I knew something I'd tell you." It was true, I would have told her.

She nodded. "Yes," she said, "I know you would tell me. You understand things." She had a moment's hesitation, then held out her hand. "Don't you want to shake hands?" she said. I shook her hand and she said, "Forgive me. I really would like you to forgive me."

Then, I don't know why, I asked her for forgiveness too.

Someone called out her name. She turned to me one last time

before walking away. Then the crowd overflowed her glasses and she was lost in the middle.

I knew I would see Arianna again. I sensed it. It was one afternoon, a week later. She was walking idly along Via Frattina, window-shopping. I'd just left the newspaper and was headed back to the hotel on foot. She saw me.

"I can't believe it!" she said excitedly.

"Yes, you can," I said. "I survived."

"I'll never forgive you," she said. "What have you been up to?" she went on, grabbing me by the wrists. "Let me see. You don't even have any scars." Then she looked at me closely. "I'm pleased to see you, *do you know that?*"

There was a different tone to her voice, but I recognized it. I would have recognized it among a thousand voices, after a thousand years, in whatever world I found myself. We were silent for a moment, looking each other up and down. She was beautiful, of course, but her style had changed, and she had changed too. She was wearing a calf-length dress and a silk blouse with a black bow at the chest. Her hair was gathered at the back of her neck and her big eyes devoured my face. She was calm, without conceit, and somehow recalled the women you see in old sepia photographs.

"How about a pick-me-up?" she said.

"I've quit drinking."

"Again? That makes it a vice," she said, walking into the bar opposite. She ordered a sherry and thanked the bartender with one of her smiles. He was elderly and reminded her of Signor Sandro.

"Sandro's not around anymore," I said. "He's retired." She asked where he'd gone and I said the first thing that came into my head—an old hotel in Stresa.

"Let's not name names, please," she said. "What are you doing?"

"The same thing," I said. "How about you and architecture?"

"I love the Romanesque," she said innocently. "*Why?*" Then we started to laugh, and we left the bar to continue window-shopping. "You remember how I liked to think I could buy the clothes?" she said. I remembered. "I'm bored with it now, but he wants me to dress up, always dress up!" she said impatiently.

"Do you love him?" I said.

She said they were getting married at the end of the summer. "Good."

"Why do you say *good*? You, of all people, should say *bad*."

"Bad."

She shrugged, left me high and dry, and walked into a store. I realized I would never love another woman in my entire life. I followed her in. She was looking excitedly through the dresses hanging on a long rack. "There's never anything here," she said, completely ignoring the salesclerk. Then she walked out and went into the store next door.

We went through six or seven stores before she decided on a red dress with one hell of a price tag. In her purse she had a check-book as thick as a finger. In many of the stores, given that she was asking me to advise her, the clerks looked to me. "This afternoon will cost me my life!" she said, laughing. "He's so jealous!"

"In that case, I'm leaving," I said.

"Why?" she said. "I'm not afraid of dying anymore. And anyway, it would be so romantic!" She grabbed hold of my shoulder and pressed her cheek to it. "Your smell," she said. "You always smell *so* good! Some of it's the smell of your car. Do you still have it?"

"Yes," I said as fragments of the previous year started to rain down on me. In a moment I was buried in an avalanche of forgotten emotions, memories of my life with her in the last summer of my life. I didn't say anything else and she too was silent but must have been thinking of the same things because when by accident our hands touched they remained clasped. Her hand in mine was very small and very cold. Around us people's faces had become blurred, were just bright patches above their shoulders. "Listen," I said, "let's go to my hotel and slash our wrists."

"If we really do need to go to a hotel, we can do something more amusing there," she said. "Aren't you in that apartment anymore?"

"No," I said. "I left it. And besides, it wasn't the same anymore."

"Of course," she said. "I wasn't there." She'd stopped in front of a bookstore. "I'd like to buy you a gift," she said, "but not a book. Something gray, to match your eyes."

"No," I said.

"Please!" she said.

I shrugged and she started dragging me from one store to the next until she found a gray silk shirt.

"Do you think he can afford it?" I said.

"Oh," she said without taking offense, "he can afford a whole lot of things. As long as people buy paintings, at least."

"Especially bad ones."

"Yes," she said, after thinking this over. "They are bad. But he knows that."

"And do you think he can afford these too?" I said, pointing to a pair of pants with silver arabesques. They were the most fucked-up pants I'd ever seen.

She started laughing. "I think he can afford a few pairs," she said. "Do you have anything against the ones with red arabesques?"

I had nothing against the ones with red arabesques and we bought them. Then we went on to buy a pair of English shoes, two dozen Chinese ties, complete with dragons, and a pair of cardinal red slippers.

By the time we left the store we were loaded down with packages. Every now and again we would lose one and there would always be someone to point it out until Arianna finally turned furiously and told them not to bother us, that *we* weren't the kind of people who picked things up off the ground.

"A blue smoking jacket," she said, stopping in the middle of the street and looking up above the roofs, "the same color as the sky."

"It'll be hard to find one," I said.

"Then let's wait for sundown," she said. "I saw a pink one on Piazza di Spagna. What would you say to a solid silver cigarette case with your initials? Or else a gold key ring for the car?" she said. "You know, those awful ones with the name of the make on them?"

"As long as it's gold," I said. "Otherwise, the car won't start. But I'd prefer a pipe."

"Why just one?" she said, walking into a tobacconist's.

We chose seven, one for each day of the week. For some mysterious reason, the one with the inlaid bull's head made her double over with laughter.

"What about him?" I said. "It seems impolite not to bear him in mind. Do you think he can afford a box of cigars?"

"Two," she said. "Don't be a skinflint."

"What time is it?" I said, indicating the little gold watch she had on her wrist.

"It's terribly inaccurate," she said with a grimace. "But it's teatime anyway."

We weren't far from a very elegant tearoom, but we couldn't go somewhere like that loaded down with packages, so we called a taxi, put the things in it, and sent it to my hotel.

"And we can't have a proper tea without a dachshund," I said, stopping outside a pet store with a dachshund in the window.

"Yes," she said, enthusiastically. "It looks sufficiently repugnant." She strode resolutely into the store. "Give me that tyke," she said. The tyke cost a whole bunch of money and had a more complex family tree than a count of the Holy Roman Empire. He was no more pitiful than most dachshunds and he walked behind us, a little scared of the traffic.

The tearoom was full of old ladies laden with jewels. We ordered two teas with orange and every kind of brioche and biscotto they had. There were even madeleines.

"Let's dunk them in the tea," I said. "Did you ever finish *Swann's Way*?"

"It's the only thing I read all winter," she said, giving a madeleine to the dachshund. "Every now and again I tried to read some of it to him aloud, but it bored him *so* much!"

"They're very good," I said, taking another madeleine. "Just like they used to be."

"Of course," she said. "This is the only place you can find them these days."

"They're getting harder and harder to find."

"My darling, the world is closing in on us! What'll become of us?"

It was a game we knew how to play.

I said I could see it all. "We'll meet secretly in tearooms until I find a very rich old lady, kill her, steal her jewels, and escape with you to Vienna."

She didn't smile but made a face. "Even old people aren't the same as they used to be," she said. "You should see him when he dresses like a hippie." She pushed away her cup. "These madeleines are disgusting," she said, putting her plate down in front of the dachshund. "Do you think they'll take a check in this joint?"

I called the waiter and repeated everything to him in detail, about the madeleines, the joint, the check. He listened to my words, pursing his mouth a little, as if he were tied to a pole and we were throwing rocks at him. He wouldn't accept the check and called the manager. We handed over the dachshund as payment and left while the ladies looked on glassily.

"Oh," Arianna said, collapsed in the backseat of the taxi taking us to my hotel, "I haven't enjoyed myself so much since he slipped on the steps of the villa and broke his leg." That's what she said, while I was thinking there was a God in the world after all. "This afternoon was so boring to start with! He doesn't like me ever to laugh, doesn't like me to cry, I never know what to do with him! I'm so unlucky!" She was despondent, and when I put my arm around her waist she took refuge against my chest. "God, how I loved you," she said hoarsely. "How I loved you," she repeated, giving me lots of light kisses on the lapel of my jacket.

"You always denied it."

"I was *so* stupid! I was scared of everything, even words. Where is this hotel?" she said, still covering my jacket with kisses.

"I don't know if you'll like it. It's very modest."

"Oh, I love modest hotels. He always goes to the posh ones. Are there hookers?"

"On Saturday and Sunday," I said, and she asked how I managed on Saturday and Sunday. She couldn't bear not knowing how I managed on Saturday and Sunday, she said, kissing my lips with those kisses of hers, as light as rain.

"You're drunk on tea," I said. "They're terrible, these tea binges!"

"Yes, if you say so, you must be right. God!" she said loudly. "I don't have any ID. Will they let me in to see you?"

But the lobby was empty, and we climbed the stairs to the top floor. The first thing we saw when we walked into my room was all our packages heaped up on the bed. I went to the window and opened it. You could see the roofs, the trees along the riverbank, the summits of the churches. In the distance, black clouds were massing in the darkening sky. I felt her arms around my chest and her head leaning against my back. "You've lost weight," she said. "I only just noticed."

"Don't you have any records?" she said, loosening her hair in front of the mirror. I found an album of old songs from the previous year and put it on the portable record player I'd brought with me from the apartment overlooking the valley, and Arianna went and sat down on the bed, pushing the packages off onto the floor. When I turned, she slapped her hand down on the blanket. "Come here," she said, making room for me, "I want to smell you." We lay down, side by side. She kept smiling. "I want to kiss you," she said as her mouth descended toward my neck. I felt her fingers loosening my shirt, then felt her mouth on my chest, moist and cool. Through the window I could see the sky losing color.

She was fiddling with the buckle of my belt. She unfastened it and continued kissing me, then I lifted her head, moved it away, and started undressing. She also undressed now, throwing her skirt and blouse on the floor. The pale marks left by her swimsuit were still on her body. She jumped on the bed, laughing. Then she stopped laughing and her voice grew somber as she hurriedly murmured words she had never said before. I turned and kissed her hard. She fell silent, and when I put my lips on her breasts she froze, listening. Then she started again with those hoarse words and my anger turned into the languor I had so long looked for with her. She felt it too and laughed, pressing her belly up against mine.

"Now," she said hurriedly. "*Now!*"

The sky was dark when I stood up to restart the record player. "I like the songs," I heard her say. "I'm so fed up with that damned Bach."

Her voice glittered in the darkness of the room, but there was something different about it. It was like hearing an instrument whose clear voice was pervaded by the hidden rasp of tortured strings. I went to the window. The clouds were looking down on the buildings and a few drops of rain were falling. On the street, people were hurrying along and from time to time you could hear the slam of shutters being lowered.

"It's starting to rain," I said.

"You're sad," she said. "I can tell you're sad."

"No," I said.

"How unlucky I am," she said. "I always make the wrong choices. I'm going home now, and I'll throw all these packages in his face."

"No," I said again.

"Why not?" she said, her voice starting to quiver.

"We can't afford it," I said. I felt she was mine. I had never before felt that so much as I did now, when she was someone else's. What lousy luck. I knew what it meant, that she could only belong to me when she was someone else's. *When she too was a leftover.* She started crying, silently. "Don't cry," I said.

"At least you let me cry," she said angrily. I went to her and sat down on the bed. "I'm ashamed," she said. "I'm so ashamed. I make love like a hooker."

"Don't be stupid."

"No, I mean it. He taught me how, he's always going to hookers."

I didn't say anything. We were so old, it was so late, everything had gone so badly.

"Graziano's dead," I said abruptly. "Did you know?"

From the darkness came a moan and her voice broke into desperate weeping. I knew immediately that it would never again be as it had been before. It was the only thing I thought, that I had broken her voice for good.

She wept for a long time, clutching my hand, while I thought about her now dead voice. Then gradually she calmed down. "I want to go home," she said.

On the street, the rain poured down with a noise like something that had suddenly fallen. We dressed in silence, while the record continued with the old songs from the previous year. When we went down into the lobby, the doorman didn't look up from his *Corriere dello Sport*, but Arianna's face hardened all the same.

By this time, the street was already dry and we walked in silence as far as a taxi stand. When we got in the cab I realized I couldn't leave her like that. I wanted to explain, to tell her something, but even when we were in the cab, surrounded by traffic, and I'd put an arm around her shoulders, I couldn't think of anything to say. Then she let herself go and laid her head back on the seat, terribly tired. "All in one year," she said. "It's such a short time, one year." She closed her eyes. "Sometimes," she said, "I wish I could go back to the clinic, but this time I wouldn't want anybody to come and get me."

"I would."

"Yes, you would," she said. When the taxi, having managed to extricate itself from the traffic, stopped outside Sant'Elia's villa, she wouldn't kiss me. She got out in a hurry, in that conceited way of hers. She opened the gate and I saw her run up the steps, press the bell, and stand waiting, surrounded by the scent of lilacs. She never turned around. Then she went in.

I looked at the taxi driver, who was asking me where we should go. I wasn't far from the hotel and felt like walking, so I paid him and set off on foot. A few drops were falling again and the city smelled of dust.

The next morning I went out, intending to go to the newspaper office. During the night it had rained again and the air was clear and fresh. When I found myself stuck in the traffic along the riverbank, surrounded by the clamor of car horns, I looked over at the trees. Their leaves were coming back. Soon, I thought, it would be summer and then fall and then winter and then again spring, and so on forever, or for a time so stupidly long as to seem like forever. What was I going to do? I suddenly knew that the time had come to get the hell out of there. They all got the hell out, sooner or later. The first rule was to not be an exception to the rule. I turned onto the first clear street and drove back to the hotel.

It didn't take me more than an hour to pack my bags. I used three suitcases, one for my clothes and two for my books, the ones I never left behind, the ones I always took with me when I went from one hotel to another, from one place to some other place. There was the old Medusa edition of *Ulysses*, Pavese's translation of *Moby-Dick*, Conrad, and the cheap edition of *Gatsby*, yellowed but still intact. I also took *Martin Eden*, Nabokov, old Hem, the poetry of Eliot and Thomas, *Madame Bovary*, *The World of Yesterday*, Chandler, Durrell's *Alexandria Quartet*, Shakespeare, Chekhov. All in two suitcases.

"It's always like that," I said to the doorman when he asked me if I was leaving. "It's the best ones who leave." He helped me put the cases in the old Alfa Romeo. He didn't like to see me go because now he would have to buy his own copy of the *Corriere dello Sport*. I compensated him by giving him all of Arianna's packages, which I had left in the room. It occurred to me I should phone the paper to say good-bye to Rosario, but I didn't feel like having to explain myself. I decided not to say anything to anyone. I would write later and ask them to send me the money they owed me. For now, I had enough for the journey and to get by at first in whichever place I ended up. As to what that place would be, I hadn't the slightest idea. I started to think about it as I drove at random around the city, saying good-bye to her. Basically, I didn't hate her, but I had no regrets and that made me sad. I looked at the flights of steps, the churches, the open-air café tables, and none of it mattered.

I got onto the highway that orbited the city and drove along it, reading the names on the signs, but one place was as good as another, so I limited the choice to north or south. I chose south, only because that's where the sun was, and I'd be able to drive alongside the sea, going the same way I'd gone when I went to fetch Arianna.

I drove until the signs with the word *Rome* on them became increasingly rare, then stopped for gas. The landscape was different. I had seen it burned by the sun and now it was green, gentle, swollen. A fabulous morning for traveling.

The closer I got to the sea, the milder the climate, and after a while I rolled down all the windows. When at last the sea appeared, it occurred to me that I'd like to go for a swim in the bay with the fortress.

After another hour, there it was, magnificent, even bigger and more desolate than I remembered. There must have been a coastal storm, because the beach glittered with wreckage and sun-blackened pieces of tree trunk. On the right, the Saracen fortress towered darkly and the stony mountains stood out against a harshly blue sky.

I left the old Alfa Romeo and walked through the scrub. The beach was full of fruit crates, loose planks, cans, and lots of rotted flowers. I reached the water. It wasn't cold. So I went back to my old Alfa Romeo and started to strip. It was when I slipped my shirt over my head that I realized this was the most beautiful place I'd ever seen and that I wasn't going anywhere else, that there was nowhere I could go except here. I sat down in the car, lit a cigarette, and smoked, thinking of how to accomplish the only thing it remained for me to do.

The hardest part was stopping myself from swimming. I thought immediately of the suitcases. The two with the books weighed a ton and I would have to take them one at a time if I wanted to carry them out to the edge of the backwash. I looked for two pieces of rope in the trunk of the old Alfa Romeo. I found only one but managed to cut it in half by rubbing it against a fender.

I was about to close the doors when it struck me that I didn't want to do this in my swimsuit. So I searched in the suitcase with the suits, took out the white one, put it on over my bare skin, rolled up the pants, and walked down to the beach.

I had some difficulty tying the second case to the other wrist, but managed it by using my teeth to help me. I managed to lift the cases. They were heavy, but it was fine for them to be heavy, because otherwise they wouldn't serve their purpose or would make things more difficult.

I went in. The water was cool around my heels. I looked at the bay, the two great arms of the bay blurry in the sun. I was at the end of my tether, truth be told.

That's all.

Like I said, I don't blame anyone. I was dealt my cards and I played them. Nobody forced me. I have no regrets. Sometimes I think about how my life would have been if that morning when it all started it hadn't been raining or I'd had money and all the rest in my pocket, but I can't imagine anything in particular. What I do think about is my city, our city. I think about the trees along the river and the summits of the churches against the sky. I think about Graziano's movie and the notes that Arianna stuck to the door in the hope of giving her days some structure, I think about my youth, now ended, and the old age I won't have. I think about all the things unrealized, the children stillborn, the angels, the loves only imagined, the dreams crushed by the dawn, and I think about the things that are dead forever, the genocides, the trees felled, the whales exterminated, all the species that are extinct. I think about the first fish that survived being abandoned by the waters, that struggled and gave birth to us. I think that everything leads to the sea. The sea that welcomes everything, all the things that have never succeeded in being born and those that have died forever. I think about the day when the sky will open and, for the first time or once again, they will regain their legitimacy.